I0456981

# Magic And Secrets

## Mary Catelli

Published by Wizard's Wood Press, 2015.

MAGIC AND SECRETS

**First edition. June 21, 2015.**

Written by Mary Catelli.

# The Wolf and the Ward

"How good to be out of the forest!" Mistress Nell raised her face to the sunlight. "Even for us—but you, you must be glad indeed, to see the duchy."

Charity nodded, knowing Mistress Nell would take it as eagerness. The merchant train wound along the dusty road. To either side, ditches spread, choked with wildflowers in yellow and purple. Ahead, a village had fields and pasture, and a hill with a manor house, where she would be delivered like any package. Her hands twitched. If she could be delivered.

She wondered whether the merchants would leave her in the road if not. They might. The coins had only paid to bring her here, not to bring her away again.

Chickens squawked from the caravan's path. A pig lumbered aside, and children turned from play to stare, curiously.

"You will impress Lord Martin with your manners. So chary with words, not gabbling all the time." Mistress Nell laughed. "Fine one to talk, aren't I?—gossiping my head off—but he will be taken with you. Lovely manners, lovely face—you have beautiful blue eyes."

Charity smiled sadly. And black hair. Like a wild beast's, other girls said. Mistress Nell might dream of a poor orphan girl from tales, but she should have noticed that Charity did not look like the tales. And a rider must have broken off to ride to the manor house, for men already rode for the caravan from it—she looked down at her hands and waited. Her horse clopped over the bridge with the rest.

"Over here, Lord Martin."

Charity cringed.

With the merchant came a man who held a familiar letter, its seal broken. Dark, tall, and lean, his features sharp—she had remembered his looks. He wore somewhat richer clothing, with rings glinting on his hand, and had grown plumper, smoothing his edges.

Not as handsome as before, said an irreverent thought. Charity looked down. Still entitled to disparage the daughter of a shameless braggart. When Lord Martin had been a page, there had been a problem with his steed—or so her father had claimed, and bragged of having helped him. She had not heard all of it, but she had seen the scorn on Lord Martin's face.

Now, he could disclaim her wardship.

"His daughter." Her father's story flooded from the merchant. Lord Martin listened without so much as blinking, with not a hint of distaste in his face, however much she studied it.

Did I imagine it? Charity wondered. She swallowed. The way he looked from Father, the derision—the shame I felt?

Lord Martin said, "You favor Sir Arnold in looks."

His voice had not changed. Charity bobbed her head and murmured something. Not, though it was true, that she looked more like her mother.

"I will commend you to Lady Blanche. The duke's house has a place for a gently reared lady."

She curtseyed, which was mannerly and hid her face. She wished he had laughed in her face. Then she would have known what was happening.


Lord Martin warned his captain, Godfrey, that after her long journey, they should not set a hard pace.

"And watch for the bandits. They've tried to take hostages."

Godfrey, his face unreadable, nodded. "This way, m'lady."

Charity sent her horse after his. She told herself that all was well, that it was one thing to refuse her as his ward, but having taken her on, he could not repudiate her again.

It still did not quiet her nerves.

Men-at-arms closed about them. Within minutes, the greenwood surrounded them, hiding the village. Birds sang, now and again.

"Watch for bandits." Godfrey snorted.

Charity glanced at him, but his gaze was on the road ahead.

"Gone to hell since the wolf. But do what we tell you, milady, and we'll keep you safe—from wolf *and* bandit."

Charity murmured her gratitude.

"What'd you tell her that for?" said a man-at-arms. "Wasn't the wolf. Was the fire."

Charity glanced at him.

"Fire nearly burnt Lord Martin alive." He shook his head. "Never the same since, everyone can tell."

"Not everyone," said another, spitefully. "Lord Martin can't tell. He thinks he's the duke's right hand."

"He's been a good master, Hugo," said Godfrey. "He's always been. . . strange. Vanished for days. And you're still here." He kicked his horse's sides; it surged ahead.

"If the duke," said Hugo, his voice low, "worried 'bout the duchy as much as 'bout his friend, we'd have no trouble. The wolf can't be to blame for it all. Can't cause trouble with the crops, can't make wells go bad—"

"A devil-wolf," said another man. "Magic gets loose, everything goes wrong. Bet you it caused the fire."

Charity nodded meekly. Dappled sunlight fell on the way as a breeze tossed leaves, and they rode about a bend. She could tell them something else strange, but if Lord Martin kept his secrets, so would she. Especially as no one would believe her.

And she should not trouble herself about this wolf. It was the duke's place to attend to a peril so fraught with mystery. Not hers. It would only draw more gazes to her—her curiosity had done that before—and a minor little maiden could hardly prosper then.

Their horses clopped on.

Soon boughs spread so thickly overhead that nothing grew beneath, and the dead, drab leaves swamped the forest floor where no earth could be seen, and nothing grew. A squirrel skittered through the dead leaves, and Charity let out her breath. She doubted the wolf caused forgetfulness.

Lady Blanche, she reminded herself, turning her gaze back to the road. A castle needed women to sew, spin, or weave.

She wished she had asked how long the journey would be.

The road went about a bend, up a slope, and then down into a hollow. Here, brush pressed in from either side. The silent guards pressed about her, watching the trees, unnerving her. Every birdcall had Charity stiffening and forcing her hands to slacken again. Her horse pranced from the motions, and she wished she could see enough of the sun to guess how much time had passed.

An arrow whistled through the company. Swords sprang out, and men leapt to the fray as if they had forgotten her. Charity bit her lip. Stay out of the way, she thought as her heart hammered; the most foolish maiden would know enough to do that. But robbers appeared all about, leaving no corner to hide in. Her horse snorted, tossing its head. She patted its neck, trying to calm it rather than make it realize how nervous she was.

A man fell before her horse. An arrow had sliced through his arm, and blood spouted, splattering her horse's legs. The horse reared, whinnying, and bolted into the woods. Branches slapped at Charity, and she clung as best she could. Shouts echoed behind her, but her horse only ran faster, losing them behind her, drowning the sounds of battle. She ducked under boughs, until the horse swerved beneath a branch too low for her to dodge.

The ground struck her back. She rolled and lay face down and aching in the moss.

The hoof beats faded, and faint sounds of battle reached her. Fighting for breath, she felt where the bough had struck, and that the moss had been dotted with acorns, but she pushed herself up to her knees. Nothing refused to move.

Something crashed through the brush, and Charity froze.

An unkempt man stumbled onto the horse's track. Blood oozed from his left shoulder, and he held a knife that glittered and bore blood. Charity took in his ramshackle clothing, the filth, the ragged hair and beard, and scarcely dared to breathe. A smile split his face, and the knife rose.

He can not mean to attack me here, Charity thought, scrambling back; Lord Martin's men must be on his trail.

He came closer. Her stomach lurched. He could hold her hostage, and perhaps he could drag her with him.

She clambered to her feet. Ferns pressed against her legs, her breath was too short to scream, and she heard no other footsteps.

A growl came from beside her. Color leeched from the bandit's face, and Charity glanced sideways. A charcoal-gray wolf stood among the ferns. With yellow eyes, it stared at the bandit, and all its teeth showed.

Charity's heart seemed to stop in the dead silence. The devil-wolf? Her hands went to the tree to steady herself, and she felt even paler than the bandit looked.

A whimper from the bandit started her heart again, to hammer in her ears.

The wolf's shoulders bunched. The bandit crashed through the ferns. The wolf sprung after, and Charity stood alone in the oaks.

She still had not caught her breath. After a minute, she realized the sounds of battle had died down—and the sounds of footsteps came after. Her breath gushed out.

"Damsel Charity!" Godfrey strode through the forest. "You are well?"

"Bruised," said Charity. "My horse—"

His hand sliced through the air. "No matter."

"There was a bandit," she said, "but—" She looked at Godfrey. A wolf. She did not think she believed it herself. With all the secrets in the duchy, she could keep her own.

"—you frightened him off."

But as Godfrey led her back to the road, she wondered whether she could leave this matter of a wolf alone. It had come to look at her.

Sunlight and chatter filled the ladies' solar. Charity sat with some mending in her lap, glad of the safety, even if Lady Blanche fussed. The duke's aunt, she had learned that much.

"Such an ordeal," said Lady Blanche.

"I feel much better now," said Charity.

Lady Blanche shuddered. "So dreadful—so much has gone amiss—these bandits were not half so bad before the devil-wolf—the huntsmen swear it must hunt *them*—but they can not catch it." She shook her head. "How is your sewing coming?"

Such a calm questions. Charity held the cloth out.

Lady Blanche looked it over, at first a glance, and then a deeper study. Charity felt calmer than before; the castle did need women to sew.

"I shall give you finer work," said Lady Blanche. "Perhaps you should make something for your guardian—Lord Martin lost much of his clothing in that fire."

A horn sounded outside. Embroidery and mending were tossed aside, and women and girls surged about the windows, laughing.

Lady Blanche smiled. "The hunt returns. You may join in admiring the knights and squires, Damsel Charity."

Charity felt color rising in her cheeks.

"Oh, Damsel Charity, come and see!" A girl pulled her into the crowd of women: the duke's kinswomen, the wives and kinswomen of his men, fosterlings and wards, the women hired to spin, weave, and sew.

Dame Alyson smiled. "Consider Sir Gilbert."

"Why, what of Sir Gilbert?" said another woman. "Consider Lord Bartholomew."

Names flew—more than Charity could fix to faces. The hunters entered the castle, with their deer. A handful of women rode with them. A blond woman, vivid in a blue hunting gown and with the color high in her cheeks, laughed. Someone named her to Charity: Lady Helena, the duke's niece.

"No one could prevent her from going!"

Lady Helena perched in the window, her sewing ignored in her lap. "Your guardian is returning, Damsel Charity!"

"I thought it was the duke," said Charity, lifting an eyebrow. Lady Helena found a new woman interesting, but Charity had learned nothing from her. Then, she could not fish too openly.

Lady Helena laughed. "And where would the duke's best councilor be?"

"His best councilor!" One woman snorted. "He has given the duke some poor advice this year!"

Lady Helena shrugged. She patted a cushion on the window seat, and Charity sat beside her.

"We should take you hunting one day."

Go riding again, thought Charity. Her back ached with the memory of her fall. Then, if she put it off, she might grow too afraid to try. "The next hunt, perhaps?"

Lady Helena's face lit up. "It's tomorrow."

Her stomach felt like a cold weight settled in it—but she nodded.

In the chilly air, morning light turned the mist gray. Outside the stable, Lord Martin looked at his ward gravely. "Are you certain you are well enough?"

Charity nodded.

"There is the wolf," said Lord Martin. "I do not believe all the tales, but the beast is uncommonly cunning and fierce."

An impish thought prompted Charity. "Why, I fear no beast when you are on the hunt. My father spoke of your valor."

Lord Martin's eyes narrowed. He nodded, curtly, and strode off. Charity's smile fell. She had just insulted him—she bit her lip. He could have disclaimed her wardship.

"Damsel Charity!" Lady Helena laced her arm about Charity's waist. "You did not let Lord Martin put you off?"

Charity shook her head, and Lady Helena beamed.

"Many women used to hunt, now and again. They fear the wolf, now, though it has never harmed a huntsman."

Charity remembered how large the wolf was. "No one wishes to be first."

"It hasn't even ravaged the sheep herds!"

"It's a devil-wolf," snarled a huntsman. Charity blinked at the intensity. "It's up to something worse."

"It haunts the hunt," said another huntsman.

Lady Helena gave them a disdainful glance. "You need a good mount," she told Charity. "Better than that palfrey that ran away with you."

She had not realized how thick the forest grew here. Even the ride to the castle had not warned her.

Giant oaks blotted out the sunlight. Moss spread about her, but strides away, ferns came to her knees, on horseback. The air smelled of earth and leaves.

The trees muffled the clamor of the hunt. These were not at all the woods where she grew up, where flowers grew in spring, and maidens gathered them, where she could wander out even if she had gotten lost. No one had told her of the forests of the duchy.

And something gray moved among the ferns.

"Damsel Charity!" Lord Martin's horse crashed through the ferns, and his glance was baneful. "Such folly—especially when you are so new to the hunt—but it will never be wise. This forest holds wolves and bandits where no one could hear you scream."

Charity tried to find words, for all that her throat felt clogged, but before she could think of anything, the gray in the forest moved. It must have shown in her face: Lord Martin glanced over.

Horror contorted his face. He slapped her horse's flank and kicked his own, but the wolf leapt from the shadows. Her horse shied and bolted—not so fast as her first one—and though she clung, she looked back. The wolf sprawled with Lord Martin's torn cloak caught in its mouth. Lord Martin's steed barreled off.

A branch brushed her cheek, drawing blood. She hunkered down and tugged on the reins. The horse ran on. She tried again, telling herself it would calm in time. A branch struck her arm with bruising force. Dear God, let it calm in time!

The horse leapt a stream, and she tugged on the reins again. It raced into a fir grove.

The fourth time, the horse slowed—not entirely, passing through the firs, into a birch grove. There, she pulled again, and the horse slowed to a halt. Sunlight spilled through the pale green leaves and over the white bark. Charity dismounted before

it could bolt again. Her heart hammered, her breath came
harshly, she stank of sweat, and she had never felt so lost in her
life.

Its breathing labored, her horse tossed its head but did not
flee. She patted its neck.

A bird chirped. Her breath slowly calmed until she could hear
other sounds, like a babbling brook. She led her horse back.
Once it cooled, she could water it. Then she could search for the
hunt.

Another bird twittered, from another direction. No other
sounds disturbed the forest except the stream, babbling so softly
that she would not hear it when she walked.

She stroked the horse's neck and wondered if anyone had
noticed its bolting. Besides Lord Martin, who might have to find
the hunt himself. She looked about, seeing nothing but trees,
and not even distinctive ones. Better when she had the guards,
with no one else to attend to, and tried to console herself with
the thought that a bandit was not on her trail. She walked on,
and eyed every inch about her.

Something stirred in the firs' shadows. Yellow eyes gleamed at
her, and she froze. The horse tossed its head, but the wolf was
downwind, and it did not bolt. Fumbling a little to keep from
turning her back on the wolf, Charity tied the horse to a birch.

She inched out of the daylight and among the firs. Her eyes
adjusted to the shadows. The wolf still had Lord Martin's cloak
in its teeth, and when it saw her gaze on it, it tossed its head. The
cloth shifted. Her mouth went dry. It was trying to throw it
over its shoulders, as if to wear it—

The eyes no longer gleamed. Charity's hands tightened. The
cloak covered its back, and the wolf rose, impossibly clutching
the cloak in its paws—its—his—hands.

No longer a wolf. A man.

A tall, dark-haired man pulled the cloak to cover his nakedness. Haggard, fierce, his face was still recognizable. Lord Martin had not gone soft around the edges.

Charity forced herself to breathe. Still handsome, said one irreverent thought. If anything, more sharp-edged.

He said, every word clipped, "I heard huntsmen saying a ward of mine rode on this hunt. I see they were mistaken."

Charity fought the desire to cringe. "I am a ward of Lord Martin's. My father left him my wardship. You saw my arrival."

"I heard then, too. Who are you, and who was your father?"

She hesitated, and her tongue moved like lead. "My name is Charity. My father was Arnold of Graybridge."

"Ah, the man who helped me when I was a page."

She had, after all, remembered. Her anger rose. He had not sneered at her father, who was the braggart. "Yes."

He gave her a baneful glance.

"Perhaps you should ask of me whatever you wished to ask of your ward. Before, you seemed anxious to do so."

His expression grew thunderous.

Her hands trembled. "Or let me go and try again. Huntsmen speak of your persistence, my lord werewolf."

His face hardened. "Are you not afraid?"

"When you could have left me to the bandit? My lord, I am Arnold's daughter. I am not a born fool."

Lord Martin stepped toward her, and the cloak shifted. Charity looked away, feeling her cheeks heat. He snorted. After a moment, he said, "Your maiden modesty is safe—and I will tell you."

He sat on a fallen log. Charity sat on the fir needles. Her hands shook until she folded them in her lap, but, but—he was furious, he was determined, and neither could quite hide how wretched he was.

His voice was low. "I have been a werewolf since before I could remember." His eyes focused beyond the trees. "Every now and again, I must come to the woods and take a wolf's form."

"When the moon is full?" Charity said.

His mouth twitched. "Not so regular a measure of time. To turn back, I need my clothing." He gestured at the cloak. "This will restore me for an hour—perhaps less."

Charity swallowed. The man passing as Lord Martin must have stolen his clothing, the last time. She said so.

"And how do you know he is an impostor?" said Lord Martin, sharply.

The air was so still that she could hear the stream rippling.

"Because he did not know that my father was a braggart."

Lord Martin studied at her.

"He must have stolen your clothing," said Charity.

"Even so. His name is Oliver—a petty noble, and Duke Leonard did not trust his counsel. He left the duke's court a year ago." Lord Martin sighed. "He must have learned my secret. I do not know how, I had kept it so many years. . . ."

Charity leaned forward. Lord Martin shivered, like a horse shaking off a fly.

"He found a magician, it seems, and stole my clothing." His hand clenched on the cloak. "Then he changed his own form to mine. He taunted me that the duke would regard *his* advice as highly as he did mine."

He stared into the forest. She clasped her hands together to keep from moving.

"I should have attacked then, but I did not realize—and he called the guards."

Charity winced.

"Now he can keep me from the castle. From the duke. And he gives bad counsel, and every task he does goes badly—Leonard has to see that—but how can he believe that I would be false to him?"

At the agony in that, Charity forced herself to draw a deep breath. "Laundry?" she croaked.

Lord Martin blinked.

"Have you tried to steal clothing from the laundry?"

Lord Martin smiled, without humor. "They wash in the river, and the land around is treeless. The laundresses would summon the guards before I succeeded."

Charity nodded, sharply. "I must steal you some, then."

"Could you tell what clothing is mine, and what is Lord Oliver's, Damsel Charity? After—" Lord Martin smiled, thinly.

"In the fire," whispered Charity. She wondered if the man had laid the fire and scorned herself. Of course, he had.

Lord Martin nodded. "And he might catch you, rummaging through his chambers without leave. But if you appeal to the duke—"

Charity sat up. "Why would Duke Leonard believe a strange, impoverished maiden over his dearest friend? A strange, impoverished, *ungrateful* maiden, who speaks such slander of her benefactor? When she is the daughter of a man he knew for a liar?"

Lord Martin blinked at the last, but he spoke with easy confidence. "When we were young, Duke Leonard gave me a ring as a pledge of loyalty. I always put it away before I changed, for fear of losing it. A gold ring, with two lions, and I hid it in the rose garden. You do know where that is?"

"I—yes." Charity's lashes fell. She had never gone in there, but she knew where it was.

"Behind the yellow roses, the wall has a loose brick, where I hid the ring." Lord Martin looked grimly satisfied. "I have seen Oliver. He knows the ring, but he does not wear it."

Charity stood. "I will bring it to the duke. When I can. Lady Blanche keeps a close watch on us."

Lord Martin smiled sardonically. "'Charity never fails.'"

Heat rose in her cheeks, but she kept her voice steady and cool. "You are unkind to tease a poor friendless orphan, who did not, after all, choose her father."

Lord Martin watched her for a minute, and she could not read his expression.

She could still feel her hot cheeks; she spoke crisply. "Once I persuade the duke?"

"Two rivers flow by the castle. Where they meet, I will await you, every dawn."

Charity nodded. "I have heard that when fell magic is loose in the land, it causes ruin. Is—is his spell to transform himself. . . ."

Lord Martin nodded grimly. Then he was gone, and the wolf wriggled out from beneath the cloak.

Charity drew a deep breath and forced herself to think. A pity she had to leave the cloak—all that spinning, weaving, and sewing!—but she could not warn Oliver that she knew, or explain how she had found it without warning him.

Behind her, the horse snorted, but the wolf did not vanish into the woods. She watched him.

He crept forward. When she did not flee, he pressed against her leg. His gray fur was rough even through the cloth, and his muzzle pressed against her fingers. The horse stirred, and the wolf fled into the woods.

A hunting horn sounded. Oliver must have mastered his horse while she listened.

Lord Oliver, she told herself. His knavery was no excuse for ill manners. She retreated to her horse. She had best think of him as Lord Martin, and the true Lord Martin as the wolf, or she would call him by the wrong name, and then she and Lord Martin—the wolf!—would be lost.

She mounted, quickly. She could not let them find the cloak near her.

Every step her horse took, she felt Lord Oliver's gaze. She kept her gaze down, but her mouth was dry with terror.

"Really," said Lady Helena, "you act as if Damsel Charity had summoned the wolf to her side!"

"She played the fool," said Lord Oliver, "getting away from the hunt. And if she continues. . . ."

Lady Helena, with a sniff, kicked her horse's sides to come alongside Charity. "Really, Damsel Charity, your guardian—"

This could go on forever, and draw more and more gazes to her, when she needed to act in secret. She raised her head. "I do not think I will hunt again."

"You *humor* him," said Lady Helena scornfully.

"I should be glad to humor my guardian."

Lady Helena snorted. Charity pondered any way to throw the conversation to the garden. She glanced up. The sky was clouding in, and in the west, the clouds piled up dark and thunderous, and so she could not manage today, but it would not rain forever.

She glanced meekly down again. Her guardian snorted and rode on. She let out her breath. Lady Helena did not look ready to ride off.


At the window, Charity looked up from her sewing. Outside, sunlight gleamed on the greenery, and blossoms in red and white—and yellow. Lady Helena had loved to talk of the garden and the games they could play in it, and the hours spent sewing there. The more fool her, to listen. Rainy days had kept them in, but now that they had sun, no one proposed it, and roses and lilies blossomed below, as far off as if they were on the moon.

She bit off her thread as Lady Blanche walked from woman to woman, until she reached Charity.

"Your work is as fine as always," Lady Blanche said. "No need for me to look it over."

Charity bobbed her head and stiffened her courage. She could not wait forever, even if word might get back to her guardian.

"Lady Blanche, Lady Helena said that sometimes we went into the garden to sew."

Lady Blanche hesitated. A girl bounced up. "Oh, yes, it's a lovely day." All about the sewing room, a chorus rose.

"I don't think," began Lady Blanche, and the voices complained.

"We always go to the garden, and we haven't—it's not like the frost isn't long gone."

Lady Blanche threw her hands in the air, and women and girls thronged to the stairs. The sweetness of flowers reached them on the steps. Outside, roses blossomed about them: pale red, sweet and tiny white, vivid pink. And yellow, the bush Lord Martin— the wolf—had meant. Only one bush, though enormous.

Women spread over the benches and on the turf. Charity sat on the grass with others her age. She was not close enough to look for the ring, not even to see if any bricks looked odd.

She looked at her sewing; the stitches seemed to make no sense. Lady Blanche would ask why she rambled into a rose bed, and worse, the women would gossip. If her guardian knew, he would guess it had to do with the wolf.

But she remembered Lord Martin's haggard face.

She took another stitch. She had gotten them here, and the ladies laughed and chattered among the greenery. If it continued fair, she could suggest it again in the days that followed. Perhaps she even ought to forbear on the first day, so there would be nothing for her guardian to hear.

Laughter echoed from the stone walls. Children scrambled into the garden: the duke's youngest three and a dozen fosterlings. The oldest girl officiously announced that they got to go into the garden, too, and indulgent smiles spread about the women. A ball emerged from the nurse's hands, and the children chased it.

A minute later, the ball flew, and Charity called, "Dame Melisande!" The woman started, but the ball still hit her face.

"Lady Elise!" The nurse stood over the child. "If you can not behave yourself, you will not be allowed out in the garden."

The little girl's face took a mulish set, and the nurse shook her head.

"Come back inside," she said, her voice ominous.

One boy looked panicked. "A lady could play ball with us. The rest of us."

Charity's thoughts flew to where the ball could land after an ill-judged throw, but Lady Helena tossed aside her sewing first. "I would love it." Lady Helena smiled. "Better punishment for Lady Elise than for all the children to miss it."

Charity sighed as softly as she could, and tried to sew.

Moments later, the ball fell here and there again. Then it flew from a hand, into the yellow rosebush. Laughing, Lady Helena went after it. The briars snagged her hair and dress, and she fought her way out again, holding the ball.

Charity looked at her sewing. Lady Helena could not have searched the wall. Perhaps the gardeners had not pruned since Lord Martin had left the ring—

She stared but did not see the cloth. So, I will sit on a cushion and sew a fine seam, watch Lord Oliver's spell ruin the land, and never give Lord Oliver reason to regret my wardship. Lord Martin will molder in the forest, finding that his first judgment of my trustworthiness was, after all, sound. And I will have a secure place in the duke's household, sewing. She finished the piece and stood.

Lady Blanche stood, deep in conversation with an elderly dame, about the feast of St. Crispin, and how they should have already dealt with the shoemaker for the shoes to be given to the poor that day. A strange custom, Charity thought, and then connected: St. Crispin was the patron of shoemakers.

Her thoughts drifted. Lady Blanche might set her to sewing something new, like—like clothing for Lord Martin. Charity twitched. Sewing clothing that she knew was Lord Martin's.

She glanced at the yellow roses. They filled the air with sweetness.

She had to keep the pieces. If Lady Blanche handed over each as she finished it, she would never have them all in hand. And the shoes would be the hardest part.

"It has to be done," said Lady Blanche. "I will not have the duke disgraced by failure to redeem his duties."

Charity stepped forward and curtseyed. Lady Blanche eyed her. "I sometimes helped the countess by commissioning the shoes, my lady. If you could assign me a proper escort, I could carry this duty out for you."

Lady Blanche scowled, and then called, sharply, "Dame Matilda! Prepare to go into the village." She spoke to Charity in a lower voice. "Prepare, yourself. I will give you the purse for the first payment."

Charity nodded. "Oh, yes, this piece is done." She pressed her sewing into Lady Blanche's hand. "And I was thinking." Her voice was so thin that she scolded herself. "You said earlier that I might make some clothing for my guardian. I thought I might make a suit for him." Her heart hammered. "I would like to surprise him, for Michaelmas. A festive suit."

Lady Blanche raised her eyebrows, looked Charity up and down, but finally nodded. "A suitable piece of work."

Charity swallowed. This would take longer, since Lady Blanche would expect only the finest, and even a simple suit would take several weeks. But she needed a reason to keep it all.

And shoes. She ran for her mantle.

Charity handed over the purse with a light heart. The scowling shoemaker took it. That's what happens when you think a young woman can not haggle, she thought. Then, she had felt so light-hearted ever since Lady Blanche had directed her to commission twenty pairs of men's shoes among the rest. She glanced at the purse and thought again that one pair would be Lord Martin's, to make the intention clear. And he was poorer than a beggar.

"And you expect me to keep here until the day." The shoemaker glanced about his small room.

That would not do, thought Charity. Seeing Dame Matilda about to say something, she said, "Of course not, the castle has room. We will take a batch once a—fortnight."

And God, help me, she prayed. Let him make the men's shoes first.

"What were you thinking?" Lady Blanche said. "Dragging the shoes here, only to drag them back? Do you think the duke lets the riff-raff clutter the gates, waiting?"

Charity kept her eyes on the floor. "I am sorry, I did not think. I will fetch them, every time, if you wish."

Dame Matilda grimaced, but Lady Blanche sat back.

"I suppose... since you said..." Lady Blanche sighed.

"I should sew," said Charity. "Should I get linen for the shirt?"

Lady Blanche rose, with the keys clanking at her belt. Charity cast her gaze down. She needed Lady Blanche's good will for all of this; only Lady Blanche could unlock the stores. She had tempted her with the shoes—

Then she would not tempt her again, thought Charity, and followed her.

A man watched her from the courtyard. Hugh, Charity thought, Lord Martin's—Lord Oliver's—man. Her fingers clenched the almost finished trewes. Shirt and tunic she had finished in ten days past, but she still had to do the hose, the gown, and the hood. And she had not kept it from the women. The story of her surprise for her guardian had spread over the castle by now.

The only thing restraining Lord Oliver was not realizing why she did it.

Hugh came into the garden, to Lady Blanche.

"My lady." His bow was graceful enough. "Lord Martin sent a message. 'Bout his ward."

Charity's fingers froze on her needle. The murmur about her, as soft as a breeze in leaves, could not penetrate her frantic, scrambling thoughts, as if they climbed on ice—how had he known, what had he guessed, what would he do, however would she manage now. . . .

"My lord wants her to make clothes for orphans, at St. Nicholas's."

Her hands felt like ice.

"How great hearted! I knew your lord was generous to the sisters, but this is new munificence."

Charity's fingers tightened on the cloth. It would take over a fortnight of work to make a suit, and no more than half of it done.

Lady Blanche came over. "I know you wished to surprise Lord Martin, but obedience is a better virtue in a ward, and these are good deeds."

Charity did not stir for a moment. Perhaps she could do the rest in secret, a little here, a little there, but the ladies' solar had no secrets.

Lady Blanche started to frown at her. She found her tongue.

"I doubt I would have surprised him, with all the rumors."

Lady Blanche nodded in approval and left.

Charity looked at her sewing. Her mouth set. A few more days, but taken in bits and pieces. The women about her could see only that she made hose, gowns, and hoods for the orphans. It could take months. Her shoulders hunched. The wolf would despair before she was done. But her guardian had realized she was doing *something*, and had gone to foil her.

Lady Blanche came in, a servant trailing with the cloth.

"How old are the orphans?" said Charity.

Lady Blanche tilted her head. "Of all ages. But they keep them until they are full-grown sometimes, to educate them, if they are uncommonly wise—most they bind out when they can work as servants, but some they make clerks."

Charity nodded. "I will make clothing for older children, and then for younger ones, in turn."

Lady Blanche nodded. Charity started to eye the cloth. She had done it, she had worked out a way—but her heart would not stop pounding.

Lady Helena, her cheeks brighter than usual, came into the ladies' solar. "We nearly got the brute today."

Lady Blanche scowled. Younger women looked at Lady Helena in rapt attention. Charity's fingers moved slowly.

"You've hunted *hard* for it," said a maiden, starry-eyed.

"After it attacked Lord Martin," said Lady Helena, "the duke realized the danger."

Charity looked at the hose in her lap. Shirt, tunic, and trewes had taken two weeks. The hose had taken already more than a week. She had made half a dozen smaller hose and hidden Lord Martin's behind them, but the work was slow.

She stitched on and wondered if Lord Martin looked for someone else.

Lady Helena sat, across from her.

Charity said, "Has Lord Martin come? I would think he has the greatest desire to see the wolf down."

Lady Helena shook her head. "I think having a wolf pounce on you like that would unnerve anyone," she said, meticulously, as if fighting to keep from claiming she would manage.


Sitting in the garden was maddening. Charity bit off the thread. After weeks of a stitch here and there, putting off the other women with evasions, she had finished sewing. She could get the shoes soon. Then, she had to escape the castle.

She eyed the wall. If ever, for an instant, she had thought that she had seen a way to fetch the ring, she would have tossed the clothes aside like so many rags. Weeks had at least let her make stitches on the clothes; they had gotten her no chance at the ring.

Among blood-red roses, Lady Helena talked of wounding the wolf that morning. Charity remembered the haggard face, the lean body, and tales of how a werewolf was found by losing a paw, and so a hand. Her mouth tightened. She wondered whether he would bear the scar forever. Or at least for his lifetime, which might not be long.

She glared at the yellow roses with enough venom to have withered them to the roots. Without the ring, the only time she left the castle was to go to the shoemaker's.

She had to use that time; it got her to the town, which had no walls. Her finger traced the cloth. However early she escaped in the morning, she could not reach the rivers by dawn. She needed to hide the night long, when the town held robbers and drunkards, and the forest held wolves and bandits.

They would have a harder time finding her in the forest.

Through the narrow windows, she could see scraps of sky as they turned from gold to orange. Charity let out her breath.

Dame Matilda spoke with Lady Blanche, and Lady Blanche looked indignant. Charity walked toward them.

"Damsel Charity," said Lady Blanche. "About the shoes."

"I forgot," said Charity. "We can get them tomorrow."

"You will get them today," Lady Blanche said. "As you promised."

Charity bowed her head and grabbed the bag she had hidden Lord Martin's clothing in.

"Dear me," said Charity, "that is a lot." She eyed the shoes Dame Matilda held and added another pair, where the pile looked most precarious.

Shoes spilled over the street, some into the alleyway. "Oh, dear," said Charity. "I'll get these." She rushed into the alleyway.

Having slid a pair into her bag when they arrived, Charity did not glance at the fallen shoes. She darted between houses, over dank cobblestones, and popped out between two shops.

To the west, clouds gleamed scarlet; overhead, the sky had darkened. A church stood ahead: Our Lady of Perpetual Help. Charity let out her breath and went inside. The shadows would hide her, among other things.

In the vestibule, a statue stood, and stray candlelight lit up the gray stone. The Virgin Mary held the child Jesus, and he looked out authoritatively over Charity. She sank to her knees and closed her eyes. Bless me, protect us, and prosper my work, she prayed.

Moments inched by. The silence in the church—and outside—calmed her. In all the clutter of shoes, Dame Matilda and the shoemaker might not even have realized that she had gone yet. She stood. Perhaps she could reach the forest with sunlight enough to see, and before Dame Matilda raised the hue and cry.

Crickets cheeped in the gloom. A few stars hung like solitary diamonds in the violet sky. A chilly breeze blew over grasses already damp with dew, and barely visible in the light. Charity shivered and glanced at the castle. She had not heard any uproar, but Dame Matilda had to have gotten back with the news.

Torches appeared by the gate. Charity bit her lip. They streamed toward the town. They would search there first, but townsfolk had seen her leave. One would realize who she had been, and tell them.

She hurried into the forest. Oak boughs and trunks blocked the faint light, and she slowed. Acorns rolled underfoot.

The moon would be full when it rose, soon, but she could not linger for it. She stepped tentatively, but still her foot landed on a root and muddy ground, and her ankle nearly twisted. Her mouth tightened. She could not wait for moonrise.

Her hand brushed a tree, and she reached out for another. She had to go where the rivers met, and the rivers themselves would keep her on the way. And moonlight would pierce the trees, there, she thought in triumph.

Charity's foot slid in mud. She kept her footing, but bit her lip. Through the branches, the silver light glinting off the water was just visible, but under the trees, the moon shed scarcely more light than the stars.

An owl hooted. Charity plodded on. The bag over her shoulder weighed much more heavily than it had at the shoemakers. She picked her way up a mossy rise.

Her skirt caught. She yanked on it and heard it start to tear. Grimacing, she turned to disentangle the cloth. She would still look a fright, but she would be warmer. The brush stabbed her finger with a thorn. She popped her finger into her mouth and walked on.

The ground ahead was muddier and less sound underfoot, with reeds. Dead trees stood there, where water had drowned their roots. Charity closed her eyes for a moment. Marsh. She had go around, or the mud would eat her. Slowly, she inched along the banks, pulling back whenever the ground slid underfoot. The river vanished behind her; she could no longer glance back and see the silver.

Water babbled ahead of her, and Charity sighed in relief. She passed the marsh and looked at the river, thinking it looked odd. After a long minute, she realized: the river flowed the wrong way.

She blinked, and blinked again. No—this was the other river. She laughed, and the noise resounded over the water. It took her a minute to force herself to stop, and more to regain her breath.

I hope, she thought, that Lord Martin does not expect me to go into the marsh; he's a wolf, he can *smell* me.

Other wolves could smell her, too, and she had not so much as a knife to fight them off.

She looked about. Maples, not oaks, from the smoothness of the bark. Here by the riverside, some had boughs that went down to the ground. The footing was wet under them, but she could reach the branches.

Charity's hand bit into the bark. Lord, have mercy. Christ, have mercy. Lord, have mercy. Blessed Mary, pray for us. St. Joseph, pray for us.

Her thoughts blurred on the rest of the litany. She dug her hands more deeply into the bark, to keep awake. The moon hung near the horizon; she did not have long to wait. St. Jude, pray for us, she prayed, randomly, and yawned. St. Agnes, pray for us. St. Crispin, pray for us.

She shivered. The morning was so cold. The chill helped her keep awake—but it was so cold.

The sky turned gray: a charcoal gray, like the wolf, but gray. She laid her head against the bark, wondered when the wolf thought dawn was, and heard a whine. A wolf, as gray as the morning, sat below, its head tilted to one side. Charity started down. Her limbs ached with every move, and the bag lurched as if trying to throw her from the tree. Halfway down, she stopped and blinked.

"Stand away." She held out the bag. After a moment, the wolf moved, and Charity released the bag. It bounced off two boughs and settled on the ground. She climbed.

The wolf faced her, and she drew a deep breath. "I tried to get the ring. I could not."

It growled.

"So—" She pulled clothing from the bag, dropping the shoes on the ground.

The wolf growled.

"I didn't rummage through his room—I couldn't get there, any more than the garden." Charity flourished the tunic. "I made them myself. They are definitely yours."

The wolf made not a sound, its gaze flickering from one item to the next.

"So here you are." Lord Oliver, on horseback, emerged from the trees.

Charity felt colder than she had in the tree. Between her and Lord Oliver, the wolf snarled. Lord Oliver drew his sword, and Charity's hands clenched. She had the clothing, but as a man, Lord Martin would be helpless and unarmed, before an armed knight. Her fingernails scored her palms. If not quite so helpless as a young, unarmed maiden.

"You were a fool, Damsel Charity. Plodding through the mud, tearing cloth—a blind man could have followed you." Lord Oliver charged toward the wolf, but the wolf dodged the blow and bit Lord Oliver's leg. Blood flowed—not heavily, but definitely, and Lord Oliver yanked his horse's reins, pulling back.

Whatever we do, thought Charity, he has the sword, and we do not. The wolf inched forward, but Lord Oliver's sword was steady, and he pulled the horse away. His gaze darted about the clearing before he sent the horse charging again. Toward Charity.

She stepped back. The wolf snarled, but Lord Oliver did not look from her.

Charity realized, with sickening intensity, that he meant to hold her hostage. Her thoughts flew. She hesitated and stopped, and her breath came low and shallow. The horse came closer, and the wolf yapped, as if trying to draw her attention. Lord Oliver grabbed her; she yanked back against his grip. With a curse, he leapt from his horse to grapple her.

"I have her, you fool! Attack, and she dies!"

Charity dug her elbow into his gut and, when he lurched, sank her teeth into his hand. Lord Oliver bellowed, and the wolf leapt through the air, onto him. Lord Oliver went sprawling, and the sword fell.

The wolf darted for the clothing. The man rose, grabbing the shirt in one hand, and snatched the sword from her hand. He had the blade at Lord Oliver's throat before the other man could move.

The sound of the horses echoed through the trees, and Charity realized that, with the wolf so close, and no rider on it, Lord Oliver's horse had bolted, without her even noticing. She tried to calm her hammering heart, and tasted—she had bitten hard enough to draw blood. She spat, but could not get the taste out. And horses drew closer.

Charity glanced at Lord Martin, glanced away, and said, "Give me the sword. I can cut his throat if he tries anything."

He gave her a wary glance.

"The cloak did not last."

Grinning, Lord Martin held out the sword. She took it with care and kept her gaze steady. Lord Oliver's eyes shifted.

"Lord Oliver, if you move, I may cut your throat through nervousness."

Lord Martin's laughter was short but still rang through the trees. Fully clad, he held out his hand. She yielded the sword, and he stood over him: two Lord Martins, one leaner and harder than other, wearing different clothing.

Neither one moving with any stiffness. "Lady Helena said that the hunt wounded you."

He smiled. "Nothing grave—but now, what shall we do?"

Through the boughs, the glimpses of the sky had turned paler, and blue.

Her voice was toneless. "If he found my trail so easily, someone else will. The castle searches for me—I left last night, without telling them why."

Lord Martin looked grim.

"Some might be within earshot," Charity said. "HELP!"

The word died among the thick leaves. Nothing moved in the trees. She drew a deep breath and shouted again. Hoof beats sounded over the hill. Charity shouted, "OVER HERE!"

A score of men came through the trees, the duke in their number, and pulled up at the sight of them. Incredulous glances turned into stares, and mutters, but no one drew any closer.

She could not read the flux of emotion that washed over the duke's face, for a moment, before it was still and mask-like. The only sign of life was that his eyes had narrowed.

"So, my lords, what have we here?"

Charity felt her heart sink.

"Damsel Charity, Lord Martin's ward, if I remember—the daughter of a man who aided him when he was a page—as was I."

Charity's gaze went to the litter of leaves underfoot.

"Looking as if she spent the night in the woods." His gaze went past her. "And her guardian, twice over. I would think a maiden might find one guardian sufficient."

Charity curtseyed. "Your Grace, you are unkind to a poor friendless orphan, who did not, after all, choose her father."

Lord Martin smirked. Lord Oliver looked blank. Duke Leonard looked between them and scowled.

A chance, thought Charity. Her words nearly tripped over each other. "Your Grace, since I came to your duchy, I have spoken to two men who called themselves Lord Martin. One of them knew my father for a braggart."

"A strange tale, Damsel Charity." The duke's voice was clipped.

Lord Oliver's voice was imploring. "Your Grace! My lord!"

Lord Martin's sword sank toward him. Lord Oliver fell silent.

The duke snapped, "Let him speak."

Lord Martin's eyes closed, but he lifted the sword.

"Do not let this witch enchant you! She is in league with the devil-wolf." He pointed at Lord Martin. "A shape-shifter."

Duke Leonard looked at Lord Martin for a long time.

Charity felt cold and lost. "Your Grace, Lord Martin—the true Lord Martin—is a werewolf. It is the wolf who is your councilor."

The duke's expression was unreadable. Mutters ran among the men.

Charity quailed but spoke. "That man is another, who learned that Lord Martin may not change back without his clothing and stole it. The day I hunted, he attacked this man to steal his mantle. He was a man long enough to ask my aid. So I made new clothing for him."

"The fire," said one of the duke's attendants.

The duke's face set. He believed her, Charity thought, but he did not want to. Her teeth closed on her lip. Then she said, "And he can prove it. But not here. At the castle."


A golden ring gleamed in the duke's hand.

He stood before the rose bush, rolling it in his hand, looking neither at Lord Martin, nor Charity—nor Lord Oliver, even when Lord Oliver dropped to his knees. When he began to plead for mercy, the duke's mouth tightened, but he did not look up.

"How dare you plead for mercy when you are not penitent?" said Charity.

That drew the duke's gaze. And every other.

"You still wear the face you stole."

Lord Oliver gibbered. When no one looked merciful, he cringed and shifted, turning plumper, his hair ruddy brown, and his face nondescript. The guards went to drag him off.

Lord Martin closed the distance, to lay his hand on her arm. His voice was low. "God bless the day that your father thought he had done me a great service."

Charity could not meet his gaze.

"This is a fine mess," said Lady Blanche, shouldering her way through the crowd. "A truly honorable way to deal with your ward, Lord Martin—having her spend the night in the woods—I can not countenance—"

Charity flinched.

"Will you be in the garden after this?" said Lord Martin, and Lady Blanche stuttered to a halt. He gave Charity a sideways glance and a wry smile. His eyes were warm with approval. "It would be unsuitable for me to attend her in the ladies' solar, of course, but perhaps in the garden we might contrive a way to appease you, Lady Blanche."

After a minute, Charity smiled back.

# The Princess Goes Into The Forest

The door opened to the dim room, sending out a gust that made cloth flutter. In the gloom, things glinted, gold and silver.

Will gawked. Then he shouted, "Look at this!"

Holding grimly to the railing, Beth climbed down the rickety stairs—no one should own a house this big without money enough to maintain it—to the room. The only light filtered through one window and turned as grimy as its glass, but she gawked, too. "I thought the family did *amateur* theatricals?"

She found the cord and yanked. A light bulb's unshaded light fell on racks and shelves. To catalogue all this. . . .

"They should have sold it," Will said. "For the taxes."

The society *had* gotten the house by paying the taxes, but Beth smiled. "The family left. Hard to pay taxes in absentia."

"When was that?" said Will.

Beth hesitated. They left. She knew they had left. They had been the Wiseman family, and this the Wiseman house. . . .

"The taxes?" she finally said. "A couple years ago." She started through the clothing. Behind her, Will rummaged. Her hair caught, and she freed it from a hanger. Vicky had been right; she should have braided it before they came. She would earn her hours of public service here. This room would probably exhaust her requirement and have more left over.

At least, it was not covered with dust and cobwebs, she told herself.

Will swirled a green cape. It unfurled dramatically, and he revealed a sword, held in one hand, that glinted, a little, in the dim light. Beth raised an eyebrow. Past him, shelves stood, laden with fans, bottles of make-up, masks, and other props.

Cataloguing would take long enough if they did not play with the toys.

"Where did they get all this?" she said.

"What did they get?" Vicky's voice echoed cheerfully in the stairwell. Then she and Rod walked in, and stared.

"No wonder they vanished," said Vicky. "Spent all their money here."

"On the bright side," said Beth, "the society'll get good money for this." The rack before her held one empty hanger, but all the rest bore regal garments, in brilliant colors. She pulled a gown from it. The blue fabric had been smocked and embroidered in white and gold. She held it to herself. "The lovely princess—Elisabetta."

"The simpering princess, more likely," said Vicky. "Like a piece of clockwork. You've got the hair at least, long and *golden* and curly."

"Automata would be an odd hobby for a princess," said Beth, dryly, "but I might do clockwork."

Vicky took up a green gown that went with her red hair. "But here we can all chose the parts we wish to play. The formidable enchantress—Vittoria, who orders all things to her will, on her own, without commanding someone else do it. Who won her way with her own spellcraft, against the forces arrayed to stop her."

"How often did the princess need to stop your enchantments?" said Beth. Vicky glared at her.

"Hail, enchantress!" said Will. "I am the great captain, the master of the sword." He flourished the sword with enough ease to reveal it as a stage prop—not that any of this was real, thought Beth. "Stalwart, brave-hearted—not a fop whose noble blood or full purse win him a place—a master of the blade!"

"And of an empty purse, no doubt," said Beth, as dryly as to Vicky.

"I gained the king's favor," said Will. "Because of my sword and my skill!"

"Ah," said Beth, "but will you keep it?" She drew back with the gown. She could take a moment.

In a back corner, a screen stood, with a mirror and small table behind it. A door, too, but for now. . . .

The dress smelled of neither must nor mothballs, and went on with ridiculous ease. Beth glanced in the mirror and blinked. The gown made her face glow like pearl, and her eyes seem large and luminous. Her hair spread past her shoulders in loose curls, not even disarrayed by the dress, and seemed golden against the blueness.

"For amateur theatricals," she said.

Her hand went to her hair. She should tie it back; she would—just, not yet. She could hardly inventory in this dress, either, but first, she came out.

"Vicky's right," said Rod. "The simpering princess." He shrugged. "It's not like heroines, or heroes, get good parts."

"How true," said Will, stabbing the air.

Rod held up a doublet in scarlet and a half-mask in black. "Behold the exquisitely subtle courtier, whose cunning and craft exceed that of the plain swordsman."

Will snorted.

"Why not go for king?" said Beth, dryly.

"Too much work," said Rod.

That, thought Beth, would depend on how much the play resembled a fairy tale.

They still eyed the clothing, and other things needed to be inventoried, too. They did not even know if this room exhausted the collection. Beth walked back to the screen and tried the door. The bronze knob was dingy with age, but turned easily.

On the other side, the room held light enough to let her see, but Beth could not tell where it fell from. She inched out, onto what had to be the stage set. With its massed rows of deep green, spangled with bright flowers, the backdrop had not been done idly, but the standing trees must have taken even more work. Rough brown trunks, showing moss, with dark leaves clustered overhead. The roots almost seemed to grow into the boards.

Beth walked over the stage, under the trees, but could not find where the audience sat. She said, "They had to. . . ." Her voice echoed oddly.

"Ah, the dainty princess in the woodland!" said Will.

Beth whirled. Her skirts swished about her.

"Do you fear the gallant Captain Guillaume, Princess—Elisabetta?"

Beth snorted. "I filled out the paperwork, Will. I really am Elisabetta, but you are *William*."

"Not like this—ah, lady with hair of golden foam—"

"You studied the sword, Captain Guillaume, at the expense of rhetoric."

"Rhetoric?" His hand went to the sword hilt. "Do you prefer some courtly fop who sweetens his tongue?"

"Which one?" She tried to ease away, but he shifted forward. "There are many young men who can speak fair in the court—"

"Any of them!" he snapped. "To prefer any of them—to an honest, hard-fighting soldier, Princess Elisabetta?"

"Hair of golden foam? Do you talk like that on the battlefield?" But her breath came light and fast.

"I am far more worthy of you than those courtiers are." He stalked toward her.

She grabbed her skirts and fled through the trees. Her heart hammered, and her breath grew so harsh as to drown out her heart. The dim light hid her footing; she tripped over a tree's roots. The moss on the forest floor did not protect her from a scrape on her hand, but she heard Guillaume running after her. Elisabetta scrambled up and ran on through thickets of brush. Branches caught at her hair or skirts, but the few tugs did not hinder her, and then she heard a burst of profanity behind her.

Despite herself, she looked. Guillaume wrestled with a bush for his sword. She giggled, but the sound was feeble for the want of breath.

She ran on. She would have worn better shoes if she had known that she would flee through the forest, but the moss underfoot eased the way.

A stream babbled over stones before her—a stream too broad to leap, and the clear water showed how deep it ran. Elisabetta looked up and down it. Downstream, white and yellow irises gleamed in the shadows, and she fled toward them and the shallow water.

The flowers nodded as the stream rippled about them. Elisabetta bared her feet, gathered her skirts and dropped the shoes and stockings in the folds, and stepped carefully into the waters, stretching her leg out. The chill made her gasp, but she could not leave footprints on the muddy shore. She waded across. The flowers brushed at her arms, and the streambed squished and yielded underfoot. More than once, her heart caught, and she wondered if irises really grew only in shallow water, but the streambed rose again, before she suffered more than muddy feet and wet legs. She climbed out the other side, taking care again to avoid the mud.

She took her shoes and stockings in hand and let her skirts fall. The bush could not have held Guillaume long, and her gown did not aid in hiding, but the forest's ancient trees stood wider than any castle's pillar. She hid behind one. Bell flowers grew there, silver and gold on their stalks, and she moved with care; one ring of those tiny bells might draw Guillaume. For a moment, she thought of her shoes, but the moss was pleasant underfoot. She waited.

Profanity burst out over the water. Slowly, Elisabetta turned. Guillaume glared at the stream. "She wouldn't cross, the simpering ninny." He eyed the muddy ground, and then a lupine grin spread across his face, and he loped downstream. Elisabetta held her breath, but Guillaume strode past where she had forded, and the sound of his footfalls faded with distance.

Far off, a bird called. She waited, to give him time enough.

"Look at the jewelry." Rod pulled out a box. Even in the grimy light, the polished pieces gleamed: gold and silver, red, blue and green stones, or more likely glass.

"Better you than me," said Vicky. "After all—Roderick, the courtier must fit the fashion." She gestured over dried bottles of make-up. "The poor, hard-working enchantress—"

He laughed, putting the costume jewelry away. "As if, Mistress Vittoria, you needed such props. You could conjure them from the minds of your admirers struck dumb by your beauty."

"You flatter, Sir Roderick. It is not an enchantress's lot to be lovely, however she looks. Princesses alone hold that prerogative."

"Princesses? Mistress Vittoria, you know of the princess we—rejoice in." He hooked his thumbs in his belt. "The glorious Princess Elisabetta, who should suffer and grow humble. A proud princess brings grief to her kingdom." His eyes narrowed as if staring through the walls. "She mortifies too many of her father's courtiers."

The courtiers left themselves open to mortification, thought Vittoria. Still, like the other courtiers, Roderick thought nothing of commoners, he scorned her enchantments and her knowledge as a *trade*, tainting all who practiced it, as no better than a tanner or an alewife—but he had come to visit her. She studied his reflection in a bowl's burnished brass side. He must know that Princess Elisabetta capriciously disliked some mild enchantments and sweet-talked her father into acting against them.

And he would not know that she, a mere enchantress, could use him better than he could use her.

"There is that, Sir Roderick, but my simple arts—"

He looked at the bottles. "They look more fit for an alchemist than an enchantress."

Vittoria twitched. "Perhaps they *look* it." She uncorked one and let pale liquid drip on a metal tray—one, two, three drops. Each one hissed like a small dragon; mist rose, coiling, and metal dissolved, leaving jagged, black-edged holes. His lips parting, Roderick came closer to eye it, and flinched at the sharp scent in the air. Vittoria, smiling a little, corked the bottle. "Or perhaps not."

Roderick blinked. He stared at the whole tray, sniffed the air, and eyed Vittoria. She smiled.

Outside, gulls cried. Vittoria pulled back the curtain from the arched window. Two gulls flew against the blue sky. She eyed them and stretched out an arm. One gull lurched toward the window. Its feathers gleamed like ivory.

Vittoria put her hand about its throat and dashed it against the stone floor. With a great clatter, the body splintered into clock wheels and bits of ivory that burst over the floor. A few gears rolled almost across the room. Vittoria let her breath out. "Those clockwork makers!" She pulled back the curtain further.

The door there made Roderick scowl. Vittoria opened it, to a room lit only by a high window. His scowl deepened. That room was wide enough that its walls had to block off that window where Vittoria had caught the gull. He glanced sideways, at the innocuous blue sky—but it did not.

Vittoria gestured, and the bits flew inside. They fell, and fell, before Roderick heard a faint clatter.

"Clockwork makers!" said Vittoria. "Worse than alchemists— tradesmen! Pretending that their craft matches the arts and learning of the least enchanter in the kingdom!" She raised her head. "I show them when they *test* their craft near me."

"Even when it's the princess?" said Roderick.

Vittoria glared. He *knew* she could not. She wondered if using him would be worth the effort.

"She never dared before," said Vittoria. "Only with the potions, nothing earlier, she meddled."

Someone hammered on the door—a small but determined hand. Vittoria went to open it.

A page stopped in mid-strike. He panted for breath. "Mistress Vittoria   King Baldwin sent for you! The princess vanished in the forest! She was attacked—" The page stopped to drag down a breath.

"Good page," said Vittoria, drawing to her full height, "tell the king that I will use my enchantments to search for her, faster and farther than his men can do so. He must order that no one *dare* disturb me."

She glanced back at Roderick. His mouth set in sour lines, he bowed, deeply enough. Courtiers could learn to respect an enchantress. Her mouth curved into a smile as she stood back to let him by. So too could a princess.


Sitting on the mossy bank, Elisabetta pulled her stockings and shoes back on. Her wet foot seemed to soak them at once, but as a bird twittered in the trees, she stood and walked back through the forest. Soon, she could no longer hear the stream. Birds sang, now and again, but no wind rustled the leaves.

Ahead, men tramped through the woods. Elisabetta paused, wondering whether to hide. Guillaume had not attacked alone. Then, as she started to pull toward the nearest tree, she saw one of them.

"WAT!"

*Mary Catelli*

Wat scanned the trees. Beneath his gray hair, his face showed more lines than it had in the morning. Elisabetta ran forward, her heart hammering.

"Princess, oh princess!" Wat staggered toward her. "We tried, my lady, tried to hold them off, but when we counted the bodies we realized we failed you. We did not hold them all."

Elisabetta reached for his knotted hands. "Good Wat, you held them. Only Captain Guillaume himself chased me. Because of that, I escaped. He would not have come with such a company if he thought he could bear me off alone, and he was *right*."

The men laughed, a strange, half-choked noise.

"I gave him the slip in the forest. I do not think he will return." She glanced about. "How—how many of our men died?"

Wat looked woebegone. "Henry, my lady. Lud is badly hurt."

Elisabetta drew in a breath and let it out. Two of the men her father had added to her guard for this journey, but she thought she could recall their faces. She tried to gauge how bad the injuries were from his face. Breathing, she thought, should not hurt.

"He won't be safe here, any more than we would be," she said. "We must go on."


Vittoria struck the bowl's side. The vision of Elisabetta, gold and white and blue in the dark forest, surrounded by her servile guard, trembled. When the water settled, it showed her own chamber again.

Not so lost, after all. The princess could not even lose herself in the forest properly. And for that the king demanded that she leave off her work and search for the princess at once.

Vittoria scowled at her own reflection. Elisabetta dyed her hair, no doubt—but she had to tell the king. She stood slowly. At least, she had news enough for him to be properly grateful.

The forest was dark.

The forest was always dark, but now—it was darker. His shoulders hunched, ready to strike at any foe or wild beast that threatened, Guillaume eyed the trees, the vines, the thickets of brush and bracken. They lurked, still and silent in the breeze-less air.

He forced his breath out. He had had no choice, he had had no other way to protect himself—the king considered being his godson such an honor that his protection was unneeded, but he would act for his daughter's husband—would *have* acted for his daughter's husband.

The ground squished when he stepped. The stream dissolved into swamp. He stepped into a puddle, and sank knee-deep into mud. Water flowed into the boot, and when he tried to wrench his foot free, it loosened itself from the boot. He had to pull that from the mud, pour out the water, and put it back on, despite the drenching.

He slogged on. The forest grew so dark that he could barely see whether his footing was earth or mud. His shoulders hunched. He would show Princess Elisabetta yet. Humiliating him like this.

When the carriage trundled up to Goldbridge's gates, the first signs of sunset were gold in the west, and overhead, the sky still showed pure blue, without a single star, but Elisabetta had felt less tired on journeys that had arrived at midnight. Outside the carriage, voices exclaimed with horror.

Elisabetta stared ahead. A clock, just within the gates, chimed out hour. Butterflies flitted through the air, their enamel work glowing. She looked at her hands.

"Princess! Your Highness!" The officials at the gate asked whether she was well—all of them, tripping over each other with the words. Guards from the militia pressed behind them, and even townsfolk. She looked about and saw, just barely, the wounded men being taken off.

"Are you well? Our land longed so for a princess, an heir to our king—it would be such distress to lose you."

Goldbridge had long held its charter; it had sturdy walls and well trained militia. Elisabetta let out her breath. They would be safe here. "I am unhurt. I sent my chamberlain, Frederick, ahead to ready the royal house."

Blinking, an official said, "Yes, he came."

"Then," said Elisabetta, "my men and I can rest there, and the coffin-maker can—can—" She swallowed. "Come there."

"I can come to make shrouds," said an old woman, her face wrinkled but her dark eyes sharp. "Your Highness."

Elisabetta nodded. The coachman clucked to the horses, the crowd yielded, and the carriage rolled down the streets. The sky was only starting to show rose-pink and was still bright—they had not lingered long by the gates—but to either hand, clockwork lamplighters lit the lamps, and lamplight found many shadows to brighten. She bit her lip, marking the buildings. Half-timbered, cramped together, even favoring the same flowers in their window boxes, they looked so much alike that she still had to count to be sure of the one she wanted. If she had arrived as she intended—Theodore lived in that house, and she would have stopped to greet him.

The door opened like a clock's, and Theodore appeared on the threshold. He still moved spryly, but his grizzled hair held more white than before. He surveyed the street and, gravely, nodded to her.

Elisabetta lowered her comb and looked at the bed. Arriving, she had found that weary as she was, she could not sleep. She had managed to eat a supper, however light, but now the sky outside had grown black, the stars had blossomed in it, and clockwork watchmen called the hours in empty, echoing streets. Perhaps she could. . . .

By the door, Frederick said, "My lady?"

She sighed and turned toward him. Whatever it was, how could it not wait for morning?

"Your father the king had Vittoria enchant the mirror in the great hall; he wants to speak with you."

She laid down the comb and fought down a yawn. "I'm coming."

In the hall, servants gaped at the mirror. Its filigree frame showed her father's antechamber; still dressed for day in blue and gold, her father sat there in the great chair, with Vittoria behind him, her eyes so modestly downcast that no glint of their avid green was visible.

Elisabetta ran down the stairs. With her footsteps echoing, the servants sprang to life and scurried off. She scrambled before the mirror.

For a moment after he glimpsed her, he looked pleased. But then his face set again in anxious lines.

"My own godson!" King Baldwin leaned forward. "I asked Frederick, I could not wait—even to summon you—to know what villain endangered you, and he said my own godson was party to this!" His gaze met hers, and his voice weakened. "He claimed it was certain."

"Captain Guillaume." Elisabetta felt like ice, and her hands clasped one another, barely impinging on her awareness. "My men held off his, I fled into the forest—he abandoned his men to the fray and followed me." She swallowed. "I escaped."

The king sat back, shaking his head. "Worse, far worse, if you had not, but this is hideous enough. After I had pity on my captain's poor fatherless son! I can only be glad his mother did not live to see it. It was so much more peaceful without him—" For a moment he frowned, as if the comparison seemed odd, but then he returned to the attack. "Drinking! Gambling! And now *this*! In search of money!"

"Money?" said Elisabetta, feeling like a clockwork parrot.

"Guillaume," said King Baldwin heavily, "has done nothing but search for money for a fortnight. I can only wonder how much he owes." His voice lowered. "And where he owes it."

Moments inched by. She swallowed.

"But you need not deal with that." He sat back, and his voice grew brisk. "I will send a suitable escort—much stronger, of course—since you must return."

"No, Father," said Elisabetta, "I must stay."

King Baldwin blinked. She spoke before he could rally another order.

"I first must see to my men, and to the graves, but then—in Goldbridge, the town militia will aid my guards at need. And that would be only if Captain Guillaume even gets past the walls. To leave, I must leave both walls and militia."

He scowled.

"Let the men hunt for Guillaume instead. He was lost in the forest and may be there still. Summon wizards who know onomastics, and have them search as well."

His scowl eased toward bewilderment.

"You are his godfather. You should know his true name."

King Baldwin roared with laughter and slapped his leg. Elisabetta let her breath out. She wondered what the spying servants would make of that.

When he mastered himself again and swiped his eyes, King Baldwin drew a deep breath, and said, in a deep voice, "Perhaps it is for the best. Your uncle acted—oddly—on the news that you had survived and escaped."

Elisabetta frowned. Her father's heir, after her. . . .

The king spread his hands. "You would think you were newborn, and had just displaced him as heir, from the way he roamed about the castle looking like thunder."

Her breath came out in a gust. "I do not think he worked with Guillaume," she said.

"Neither do I think so," said her father. "But perhaps it just well that you avoid his rage."

Having dismissed his daughter, King Baldwin did not let her break the enchantment. With a fond little smile, he watched Elisabetta hurry back up the stairs, even when she was only a glint of gold hair in the shadows. Only when she had vanished behind a door did he rise, nod to Vittoria as if the courtesy meant anything, and retreat to his bedchamber. With the door closed behind him, Vittoria dismissed the image. Her eyes narrowed as she stared at the glass. Fortunate Elisabetta, to bend the king to her whims. She wondered if the princess had any notion how hard life could be for those who had to obey the king, or how much harder she made it in her carelessness.

"None of us," she whispered to the empty room, "chose our parts in this." With a swirl of her skirt, she left.

In the hallways, guards and servants shifted and subsided, seeing it was only the enchantress. Vittoria stalked onward. It would serve the princess's pride right if she conjured Guillaume

into the Nameless Tower. She used it to hide the ruins of
impudent automata, but it gained its name from its power to
hide things from onomastics.

In the great hall, where a handful of courtiers lingered,
Roderick bowed to her. After a moment wrestling with prices
and consequences, she walked over to tell him what had
happened.

"She shelters her pride well," said Roderick. "And she thinks
highly of that town of craftsmen—sheltered by their charter—"

Vittoria's mouth twisted. She had just told *him* that.

"But when Captain Guillaume *is* captured—" He raised an
eyebrow.

Her mouth pursed.

"Not to mention that you could show how enchantments are
better than onomastics."


The sky was overcast in the most delicate of dove grays.
Elisabetta, like everyone else, wore black.

She had thought Lud would survive when he reached
Goldbridge alive, but it had taken only another day. And Bredon
would be lame for life, the chirurgeon said.

"Such a scandal," said the sexton, solemnly. "All the trouble in
the land when we had no heir to the throne, and to risk your life.
. . ." He shook his head and went ahead to where the graves had
been dug.

It was half an hour later, returning from the burial, when she
thought that the sexton was barely older than she, and could not
remember those days when her father had no child, and even
then, he had had a brother.

Rain splattered the street, and she hurried inside. She had
been born only three years after her parents wed, but they had

been anxious—she had heard that so often—and it had never seemed odd before.

In the sunlight, Elisabetta walked toward the center of Goldbridge.

The great clock struck the hour. The golden sun, the silver moon, and the stars in gold, silver, and copper, moved to new places. Below them, enameled men and women danced, tiny hands and feet moving in patterns. She would never gain that much skill. Only an apprenticeship, and many years of work as a master, could teach her that much skill—and what was the point of such an apprenticeship when you would become a queen rather than a clockwork maker?

Or, at least, rather than a master clockwork maker.

She walked on. Theodore's house bore its old sign: a green parrot so old and weather-beaten that she knew the color more from memory than from sight. She knocked.

"Come in, Your Highness," said Theodore's daughter-in-law, Silvie. "My father's in the workroom."

Elisabetta nodded—as if he would be elsewhere—and walked down the hall. Her hair was already carefully tied back and netted in a lacework of metal to keep it in place.

Square, solidly build tables stood in the workroom, and sprawled over them were intricacies of wheels and springs, delicate disguises of enamel and glass, cogs and gears and more metal. Theodore frowned over a little bird, still showing all metal cogs and gears, without the enamel colors for the feathers, or even the feathers themselves, next to him. Only someone who knew clockwork could already see the bird form. Elisabetta smiled.

Theodore grunted and looked up. "Ah, princess. A sad business, this about Captain Guillaume."

Her smile vanished. The very thing she came here to avoid had struck along the way. "If I had not come here—"

"If you had not," said Theodore, "he would have chosen some other way. Perhaps a worse one. For you, for your guard, for the kingdom—" He shook his head. "Your work place is ready." He gestured at the table glittering opposite him. She went to sit there.

"Father should be pleased," Elisabetta said. "He wanted me to know the kingdom's trades, and I am learning one." She lifted her hands. "One where dainty little hands are *useful*."

Theodore smiled, but after a moment, he shook his head. "I have the oddest thoughts about you. As if you were a cog that appeared in the midst of clockwork, intermeshing. . . ."

Elisabetta blinked. "You came to court when I was—five. With birds and a lion. I snuck away to watch you work."

"Intermeshing, dear child, fitting with the cogs and springs and posts." Theodore smiled again. "Which is what makes it feel odd."

Elisabetta smiled back and built. It was so peaceful here, and yet the courtiers wondered why she left them and their backbiting for this town. She picked up a piece of ivory and considered.

"What are you making, princess?" said Theodore.

"A lily—it can bow and bend as if in the wind." It would be no match for the clock or even Theodore's bird. Then, when she made trinkets, they would be treasured more for coming from the royal hand than their workmanship. She eyed the cogs again. That did not mean she would stint on the work.

He chortled. "Child, child, already reaching for new wonders? You will exhaust what you can do in clockwork."

She sighed. "Perhaps I will. . . ." If I have time enough to amuse myself. She choose more ivory, to make the petals.

"You came quickly after the last time," said Theodore.

"So I did." She sorted the ivory by size. At least it consented to being put in order. "But an enchantress came to court. She makes love potions, from sheer mischief, it would seem."

"She does not sell them?" said Theodore.

"Only after she had used them as pranks."

Theodore lifted his hand. On his finger, a tiny yellow bird trilled its clockwork heart out. "Perhaps she meant them as advertisement."

Her mouth twisted, and she rested her hand on the table a moment, to avoid an ill-judged motion. "She should have considered what else they would do. They gave the court gossips enough tales to last them a few centuries. I persuaded my father to put his foot down." She picked up a petal and sighed. "Eventually." The weeks had been long, and she had heard enough jests about how she had turned into a terrier. She bent over the ivory, checking the size of the pieces.

"And so—the escape here."

"There were also gallants, being gallant," said Elisabetta. "I do not know why stopping Vittoria means that young idiots can plead with me to soften my heart without a love potion."

Theodore snorted, but Elisabetta sighed again. "At least they did not kill anyone while pleading." She drew a deep breath. "They said—the king my father said that my uncle acted strangely at news I had escaped."

Theodore snorted. "Your uncle's strange. You must remember that, back in the day, he was a quiet little shadow until—what was it?—twelve years ago? Then suddenly he was full of advice for the king, and confidence, and—" He scowled, and spoke more slowly. "And that he had no relatives as close—distant cousins, only—he—" After a moment, he continued more briskly, "To advise him, that was. You would have made no counselor in those days, however precociously sage you were."

He tilted his head to one side. "Do you remember? You were young."

Elisabetta considered. "Something. I was young, so the queen my mother tried to keep the king my father from complaining where I could hear. I still heard some of the grumbles."

"There—there were those who feared a regency for you."

"From that, at least, we are safe now. I will be queen or nothing."

She picked up more cogs, to go on being a maker of clockwork.


The park trilled in every inch. Birds, from brown to splendid with every gem-like color found any jewel box, some glinting in the sunlight, and some hidden among the leaves, sang on the tree boughs and drowned out the chimes of the town hall's clock.

Elisabetta smiled.

The birds stopped as suddenly as they had begun. A few trilled on, those built to sing like true birds. Or, perhaps, true birds, which still sometimes nested here. Elisabetta wandered on. A golden stag lifted its head and looked at her with sapphire eyes. A little stiff in the motions, but she laughed. "Are you a fairy-tale deer, so that a prince, hidden in your belly, can sneak into a princess's bedchamber? I'm wise to that, you know."

From behind her came a light voice. "Princess, princess, princess!"

A boy ran up—thin, in a respectable blue smock—the baker's apprentice, from the bakery next to the royal house. She stiffened even before he spoke; he could not have come to bring bread and pastry this time.

"Princess, the king sent guards!"

Feeling cold, Elisabetta nodded. Had her father changed his mind? Or had Guillaume been captured? She gathered her skirts to hurry alongside the boy.

"Your Highness!" Before the royal house, Roderick swept a deep bow.

Elisabetta stopped, letting her skirt fall from her hands. Townsfolk clumped about, looking at the guards, and talked; some were giggling, and others gravely considered, but they did not realize how odd this was. She hoped Roderick would make no more pleas about her hard heart—at least, not publicly.

Her voice was cool. "Sir Roderick, I had not realized you had joined my father's guard."

"Your Highness, how could any man stand aside during your time of peril? Why—" He waved at the crowd. "You thought this town's militia would protect you—tradesmen!—but you expected less of the nobles?"

"Am I in danger?" said Elisabetta. Breezes teased at her hair.

"Not at all. Captain Guillaume is captive—he babbled of a woman who lured him—" He shook his head.

"Strange," said the captain of the guard. "Onomastics did not find him, and no one knows what lured him to us. But it is him, without a doubt."

Roderick nodded. "King Baldwin wants him tried at once, and you and your guards are needed, to give evidence."

"Of course," said Elisabetta, thinking of the coffins. "Did you give Frederick the news?"

"It was meant for Your Highness!" said Roderick, and the captain's mouth twisted.

So Frederick had not started to pack. They might not even leave today. "We must tell him at once."

As she walked into the great hallway, Roderick came behind her. "A strange sanctuary, a town of tradesmen. They don't even call you 'Your Highness.' I heard them. 'My lady.' Even 'princess.'"

She went toward the stairs and wondered whether he would chase her about the house. "I find their simplicity pleasant. And they are good people, with good hearts."

"Perhaps they have few faults, but they lack the virtues suitable to serve a princess."

He reached before her for a door. She blinked, looking at his hand. She had seen something, or had she?

"They can not protect you properly," he said.

"They have," said Elisabetta.

"Only thus far." Roderick opened the door—not to the room, but to a stone cell lit by a high window. Cold reached out to them. While she gaped, he grabbed her wrist and hustled her in. She dropped over the threshold and landed on straw and small, hard things.

"They'll take the blame for this, you vanished in their town, and it serves their impertinence right!"

Elisabetta looked up. He—what had the town done to him?

"But first of all, it serves you right—proud princess!" He shut the door.

Elisabetta gawked at the dark wood, but before her gaze, the brown of it shifted to gray. The grain of the wood become the roughness of hewn stone, part of the wall. As the knowledge sank in, her heart hammered in her chest as if it could break through her ribs and the walls outside, stone though they were.

This could not happen. That pompous windbag could not enchant a door—

Enchant. Elisabetta groaned and staggered to her feet, and felt the bruises that were forming where she had fallen. Her stomach roiled. She wondered if Roderick had sought out Vittoria, or Vittoria had urged treachery on Roderick, but it did not matter.

She walked to where the door had stood, and her hands agreed with her eyes: no seam betrayed an exit. She rubbed her arms. Maybe he meant to keep her safe enough, maybe he meant only to attack Goldbridge with charges that she had not been safe there—but why did he want to attack the town so? Nobles objected to royal charters, but Roderick showed remarkable spite, and Goldbridge's charter was centuries old.

Unless he minded that she hid from court there.

Even that was madness. He had shown his hand. If she—her mouth tightened—if she escaped alive, he would have committed high treason for the sake of petty spite, and would suffer its penalty.

She shuddered. The folly was so great she could only wonder why she was imprisoned instead of killed at once, without waiting for the end. Had—she stared at the stone—he even *thought*?

She turned away, though only to more stonework. Theodore or someone would send her father a message by clockwork, even if Roderick did not start to accuse them of carelessness with the princess at once, but her father had searched for Guillaume for days, as hard as any search could be, before his capture.

For a moment, she wondered whether he had lied there, if Guillaume was still free, and party to this. It would be like him, but the captain of the guard had not contradicted him. None of the guard had any love for the courtiers.

Still, it took many days for that capture. It could take as many to search for her.

Her hand clenched into a fist. She should at least try to escape. She walked about the cell, pressing on the wall, seeking any gap in the stone.

Her foot hit small, hard objects. Some skittered over the stone, and she crouched to look. Across the floor, intermixed with straw, broken clockwork lay, gleaming cogs or gears lacking polish, some bent, others twisted, some merely scattered as if a device had fallen apart. Her gaze trickled over the pieces. She could not even pick out their original purpose, or even if they stemmed from one contraption. She glanced at the featureless wall, gathered a few pieces, and laid them in a pile by the wall, before continuing her circuit, inspecting every inch of the wall.

Then she came to the pile again and stared down at the brass and steel for a long time. The still air about her felt colder and more dank than before.

For a moment, she pondered whether her uncle's odd behavior might have led to this, but he scorned enchantment as fit only for commoners. And Roderick as a fool.

She knelt to gather pieces, one by one. Her thoughts felt flat and featureless, and what else, after all, could she do? Pace interminably? Stare at the wall?

One jabbed her finger, and she jerked her hand back. At least it did not bleed. She looked at it a moment and told herself if she had enough of the pieces, perhaps she could reason out what they were from, and from that, where she was.

At least it would give her something to do.

The light slowly shifted. Every now and again, birdsong came through the window, or the sound of a breeze blowing—without stirring the air within. The metallic click of the clockwork was more regular.

After a long time, she heard a different sound. She suppressed her start and turned, hiding the pile of clockwork behind her skirts.

Vittoria looked down from a door half way up the wall. Elisabetta's eyes narrowed, but she could not reach there by any means. She thought it had been plain stone before, but she had not studied the walls above her reach. She glanced behind her. It seemed that Vittoria stood in her tower, in the castle.

At least the door was far away enough that she could look without craning her neck. She straightened.

"The proud princess," said Vittoria. "Humbled."

"Your love potions," said Elisabetta, "did not draw down half the trouble that this will. A tenth. A hundredth part."

Vittoria's lip curled. "I am an enchantress, Your Highness. You will not testify against me. And onomastics will not prove useful." She smiled. "If he thinks to use them. Your father turned to me when you fled Captain Guillaume, after all."

Elisabetta looked at the enchantress's face. Vittoria's eyes narrowed. After a minute, her face set in disgruntled lines, she closed the door.

Elisabetta wondered if Roderick knew that he prevented her from meddling. She looked at the clockwork. Then, he had not brought her here to woo her; he was not Guillaume, fool enough to think this way would win her. Her mouth twisted. Although he might return, hoping to find her more amenable.

She returned to the cogs. She had neither tools nor a bench; at that, she had little light. But she had nothing else to do, she still wore her signet ring, which would make a message convincing, and perhaps she could cobble tools together. She hunted through the straw for every scrap of metal.

When she had eyed at every inch, Elisabetta walked back to the heap. Her foot struck another spring. She studied it. With all the straw about, she might have missed more, but she did not hunt them as treasures, but for use. And from the window, sunlight gleamed through golden motes; time was passing.

Elisabetta sat by the pieces. This was dangerous. If Vittoria saw it, she would react with fury. Elisabetta poked the pile, pulling out cogs. And it might only bring her danger. She did not know what the plotters intended; Vittoria might even haggle with her father for her freedom.

Then, what price would the kingdom pay for her freedom?

She bent over the pieces, and her hair fell down. She divided it into three hanks and braided it. Having not so much as a ribbon, she could not tie it back, but she threw the braid over her shoulder and set to work. Cogs served as crude screwdrivers, and in lieu of a hammer, she could knock the pieces against the stone.

And if she broke some pieces, she could hope—she glanced at the pile—that she had enough to break some.

She tapped one cog onto a pole, and the pole fractured. She picked up another pole.

Or even to break many, she thought grimly.

On the floor, a wooden plate appeared with bread—brown peasant bread, not the white bread that even a minor courtier or a prosperous merchant would sup on—and a wooden goblet, with water. Elisabetta eyed them. Vittoria was an enchantress, but if she falsified the food, she would have made the deception more extravagant. Elisabetta rose. Her legs protested, and she walked about the cell, to bring them to life, before she sat to choke down the bread.

If onomastics would not work—the goblet stopped, halfway to her mouth. This must be the Nameless Tower. Elisabetta eyed the walls. Then, despite herself, she smiled.

"How you suffer, Vittoria. You can never let me go free and unenchanted, and so you can never let the world know that you found the Nameless Tower."

She looked at the cogs she had pieced together. Half a dozen, no more. Her fingers ached from forcing together the tiny pieces, with their edges. She would labor for days, weeks, perhaps months, to build a single piece of clockwork.

She took a post and laid it aside. One every day. She would know how long this captivity lasted.

And then she gathered straw together, into some kind of bed, to be ready for nightfall, when it came. More clockwork pieces came up, for the pile.

A dozen cogs, no more, and she could do no more this day. Elisabetta sat back. Pain shot through her legs, protesting how she had sat on them. She stretched her neck and arms as they joined in the ache. She had no choice, either in working or in stopping. The reddish light shone too dimly for her to labor, and she needed her sleep. She had even drawn blood from her hands when a clumsy move had jabbed her with a cog's prongs.

After a minute, she took handfuls of straw from her bed, to scatter over the bird. She hesitated and then, as the light dimmed, moved her bed farther away, so no accidental thrashing could disrupt her work.

A week later—she had laid aside nine posts, and the work had grown a little easier with time—a bird perched on her battered finger. It wore drab feathers, the better to spy in, but Elisabetta did not know whether she had done the eyes right. She had only seen Theodore do it three times, and never thought to try it herself. Or even aspired to, some day, with more skill.

She forced her breath out. If this failed, she would try to build something else. The tower held more clockwork pieces than she had imagined.

Elisabetta lifted her hand. The bird flew up to the window and out, as easily as any automata she had ever made. She sat on the floor.

Time passed, time she could not measure. It was worse than the days when she bent over the clockwork. She wished that she had built a clock first, to measure the wait, and wondered if Vittoria would bring her meal when the bird flew back. If the enchantress realized—Elisabetta had never prayed so earnest before in her life.

Again, the food appeared. At least, Vittoria did not, but time passed, with no sign of the bird. She ate. She tried to ponder

what else she could build. If she learned nothing from the bird,
she would have to devise something useful regardless of what lay
outside. . . .

Sound at the window drew her eye, and Elisabetta jumped up.
She spilled her water, but the bird flew to her finger. With great
care, she brought her right hand to its head and pressed to either
side. Its tiny eyes dropped into her palm. She tweaked where
they lay until she looked down into them.

A scene sprang up before her: fields, pasture, and woods.
Rush-lined rivers wound through it, and here and there about it,
villages stood, none large. A gray tower stood between a pasture
filled with bleating sheep, and a wood.

"In fact, like a thousand places in my father's kingdom,"
Elisabetta told the bird. "At least. Ten thousand, perhaps." She
sat. Villages with charters, since no castles loomed over them.
The peasants were better off without nobles, usually, but she
could not know the land by the flags the castle flew, and so work
out where to send a message.

Elisabetta sighed.

The bird tilted its head. She popped the eyes back in and ate
her last bread. The bird tilted its head again. Despite herself, she
laughed. "Sorry, birdling." She ran a finger down its head. "You
don't have a stomach."

It trilled. She could send the bird to the villages. It might
read some inns' names. Then, if the inns did not have names that
revealed the village, she would learn no more.

"I need—" She breathed out the words, rather than spoke. "I
need something vivid. I do not need to know where I am. *They*
know where they are. And news of anything strange will go to
the king."

She looked over the enamel. "A bird of red and orange and
yellow—I will need them all just to get the bird feathered—
maybe all the other colors too."

She eyed the window. It was large; perhaps even she could pass through it herself. But the bird needed wings.

"Fiery flamboyant. Perhaps—a phoenix."

To make a phoenix, she had to make it burn, but she had no simpler way to ensure it drew the eye. Elisabetta looked back down, at the scattered pieces. She had heard Theodore refuse several orders for a phoenix. However good the price was, it took hard work.

She flexed her sore fingers. But Theodore had accepted one such order while she was there, and she had watched, rapt in fascination.

And she could not imagine a better signal.


A drumming sound woke her in the morning.

A steady low drum, and as she rolled over on the straw, and her foggy thoughts pushed their way through the murk, Elisabetta recognized it: rain.

She opened her eyes. The light was gray not with dawn but with cloud, and the air was colder than ever before. It did not rain in, and no water slid down the wall, but she did not whether the wind would shift. And her little brown bird—

Elisabetta whistled. The bird lurched down. More like a butterfly than a bird, she thought, critically. The works might have suffered from the rain. Because she had pieced it from ruin did not mean it lacked the delicacy of clockwork.

The cold left her stiffer than usual; she stretched. Then she uneasily glanced at her phoenix. Too little light came in the window for her to work, but if rain puddled on the floor, it would ruin her work.

She looked at her bed. Then, slowly, she shifted it under the window. If it did rain in, the straw might soak the water up. She could wear herself out until she could sleep on stone.

With that done, she walked about the room, to wear off the hours. It helped some. And with time, the tower grew brighter, though the daylight was still gray. She pondered.

Vittoria had filled the cell with shattered clockwork. If she found her making the phoenix, the enchantress would smash it. If she splintered the right parts, no phoenix could be built, not by the most skilled worker in the land.

Elisabetta looked up from her thought. Light had grown, to enough for her to work. She walked over to the parts and sorted out everything needed for the phoenix; it glinted in her hands. Then she sat beside what was left and built again, another bird entirely. Easier than the phoenix, at any rate.

Weeks later—the pile held more than fifty poles—evening came again. On the phoenix, Elisabetta happily fit in the first of the last row of feathers. She half thought that Vittoria had set a spell to deliver the meals, and then forgotten her entirely.

"What mischief are you up?"

Vittoria's voice, harsh as a crow's cry, resounded from the stones. Elisabetta started, dropping a feather, and glanced upward.

"Will *nothing* teach you humility?"

Vittoria glared from the doorway, once again half way up the wall. For an insane moment, Elisabetta thought Vittoria studied her hair, but any minute, the woman would realize that Elisabetta made things of clockwork. Then she would unleash enchantments. But one was already done and sat beside her.

Elisabetta touched her falcon. Black wings beat the air as the bird rose. She forced herself back to the phoenix; not watching, she could not know whether the falcon worked, but she needed every moment. If it failed, she could not amend it, so ignorance did her no harm. For a few, she heard only the wing beats, and the hammering beat of her heart. Her hands were so unsteady that she moved very slowly, taking up a feather and putting in place.

Vittoria's voice was even harsher. "What madness is this?"

Elisabetta put in a second feather.

Vittoria screamed. Elisabetta's hand jerked, knocking out three feathers. She glanced up and saw more red than Vittoria's hair. Vittoria threw up her hands before her face, and the falcon pecked, clawed, and battered with its wings—buying precious time. Elisabetta tried to look back at the phoenix.

Shouts resounded, and footsteps. Elisabetta's heart hammered. If the enchantress was caught with the door open—

Vittoria, her face streaming blood, fended off the falcon with one arm. "You will not—" She slammed the door shut. The falcon lunged again and was trapped with her.

Feeling weighed down, Elisabetta turned to her work. If the door had to lead here, so would the door that Roderick had enchanted, and she would have been found long since; Frederick would have had the house searched first—ransacking every inch of it, opening any door they found.

And if Vittoria were captured, she might starve.

She laid down feathers with exquisite care and sighed. She remembered Theodore's words, about a new cog in the clockwork. She knew what he had felt. Though she knew herself to be King Baldwin's daughter, though she remembered years at court, she felt odd.

Even in this gloom, even built of a hodgepodge of enamel, the phoenix gleamed like a fistful of jewels.

"Luck," said Elisabetta, severely. "It's the catching ablaze that I—well, I do not *rely* on it, but I think it more likely—"

The little brown bird chirped. She had built it to spy, the falcon to defend, and the phoenix to burn.

She shouted at the little bird, "Get out of the window," and lifted the phoenix. The black glass of its eyes glittered, its plumed

head lifted, its fiery orange wings beat the air, and it took to the
air, taking its weight from her arm. She stood, watching, feeling
the breeze and wrapping her arms about herself, waiting. It flew
toward the window, and she held her breath. She might have
misjudged the window's size, or the phoenix's wingspan, or the
phoenix might fly wrong, and her right calculations would go
awry for that.

And then, its wings brushing stone to either side, the phoenix
flew out. Her hands clasped together. If the fire would only
work as well—

Light blazed, so sudden and brilliant that even looking at
away at once, Elisabetta blinked, half-blinded. The blaze roared
in the air, and her heart hammered as she hoped, and hoped. The
stones came clear before her eyes, stained fiery shades by the light
surging through the windows.

Minutes later, the light had clearly slackened. She turned her
head slowly, wary of the light, but she could look out the window
without being blinded, and see the glory of scarlet and orange.
The roar of the fire abated, and other sounds followed—she
hoped they were shouts.

She let out her breath. And now to wait.

Her heart hammered, insanely.

She sat on the bed, more tired than her work would explain,
and minute after minute inched by, but she only drowsed when
she heard noises at the window.

She sat up.

"Don't be a fool, Hob," said one. "Richard can think that it's
no danger, but I—"

"He's the mayor, Tom," said another voice, sourly.

"Who's there?" said Elisabetta. Her voice echoed from the
stones. When silence answered, she said, "Whoever rescues me
will find the reward fitting."

"Where are you? Who are you?"

"A prisoner." She drifted closer to the window, and fretted with her signet ring. However filthy and ragged she was, she could prove herself the princess, if she escaped to someone who could recognize the ring.

"A bird," said Tom. "This big bird flew out of here."

"Clockwork," Elisabetta said.

"It—," said Hob. "Richard swore it was a monster out of legend."

"Free me from here," said Elisabetta, "and I can prove to this mayor of yours that it is, indeed, clockwork. Before granting your reward."

Elisabetta sat in the tower window and blinked like an owlet. Hills and valleys spread before her. The little brown bird had shown her truly: farmland, pasture, and forest. Sheep bleated below, and she blinked back tears.

"Uh—lady," said Tom.

"What are you doing?" A voice screeched up the ladder. Elisabetta thought it was a woman, but a glance down showed nothing and left her sick with dizziness.

"Rescuing a lady!" shouted Tom.

"Let her let down her hair, it would be more fitting—"

Elisabetta laughed, breathlessly. "I can't wait that long." She put one foot on the rungs. Tom muttered encouragement, and they descended. And descended. He never went more than a rung or two below her, and she thought he had judged her strength wisely. All the more as the descent continued, and she did not dare look down to judge the distance.

When her foot hit grass, she scarcely knew what to think.

After a moment, she put down her other foot. Then she took her hands off the ladder, drew a deep breath, and turned toward the fields and forest.

A peasant woman, of middle years, studied her. With a scowl on her weather-beaten face, she muttered to the men, "Well, she doesn't *look* like a wicked witch trapped there."

"I can explain all to your mayor," Elisabetta said. She smiled, and her face felt stiff.

"I hope so," said the woman. "It's an odd prison." She looked aside, to where Tom and Hob led a huffing man up to them. He wore a fur-collared coat, too hot for the day, and a golden badge of office.

"Well, now, Meg," he said to the woman, "what have your sons found? This time? That you thought important enough to fetch me for?"

Elisabetta held out her hand with its ring. Slowly, as if to advertise his reluctance, he looked at it. Then he scowled. The other three murmured, as if unsure that they did recognize it, but he was silent. His ruddy face managed to pale. After a minute, he took her hand in his, to inspect the ring, to make sure, and then he dropped it as if fearing to lose his own hand for insolence, and threw himself to his knees.

"Princess! Your Highness!"


"They're all but ready," said Mistress Nan, glancing at Elisabetta where she sat by the fireplace.

Elisabetta nodded. They had not lit the fire here on this pleasant day, and even with the windows open on the sunshine and fields, the stone house had much to remind her of the tower. She swallowed. She could not have left sooner; she was still a princess and had her duties.

Then, she had managed. Even with the townsfolk fussing about the simplicity of the dress and food they could provide. And now....

She stood and walked from the room. The guards hurried about her, as if they feared the strike of bandits or sorcery within the town walls. She managed a smile and hoped it did not look strained.

The captain, grizzled, with a scar on his face, nodded to her. His lieutenant, fair-haired and, she thought, of noble blood, bowed more deeply.

"It will be a long journey, Your Highness. Many towns and villages have never seen anyone of the royal family before. And wish to express their good wishes and their rejoicing at your safe recovery."

She nodded. Such fetes were part of travel.

"Why, I even hear that your uncle, who had fared to Clearwater, has hired a troupe of actors for a pageant, in celebration."

Her eyebrows went up. Perhaps he wished to dissuade her and her father from remembering her first escape.

"That will be pleasant," she said. "Actors from that town have played pageants before the court."

"First," said the captain, "we have to reach the town. And for that, we must first take to the road."

Elisabetta nodded and turned to the carriage. Not a royal one—it had not a scrap of gilt—but with large windows, she noted, so that all could see the princess within.

Her little brown bird flew within, and chirped. She smiled.


In the darkness, Roderick edged toward the cell. He should not do this; he should deny all. If Vittoria accused him, he could claim that she had used him to imprison Elisabetta without his knowledge. His mouth tightened. She was an enchantress, she might have made him do it, and then forget the enchantment that forced him, that would explain why he had not helped. . . .

Her shoulders hunched, Vittoria perched on the bed. Light from the cell's window left half of her in darkness, but whenever she shifted, it showed more of the brown, dried blood from the falcon's attack, tracking down her face where the blood had flowed like rivers.

He could claim it, but King Baldwin would not believe him. His fingers tightened about the bars.

"You were a fool."

Vittoria looked up.

"The king suspected you, no doubt, the moment she vanished. With all your vaunting about your—enchantments."

Glittering in the gloom, her eyes narrowed.

"If you kept your wits about you—but when they saw the falcon was the princess's handiwork, you were doomed."

Vittoria drew herself to sit upright, not managing to look dignified. "Have you nothing *useful* to say? Did you come here to taunt me before your own arrest?" Her lip curled. "You will find that cold comfort in a cell."

"Do you think *me* a fool? To *trust* you to hold your tongue?"

Vittoria surged to her feet so suddenly that he stepped back before he realized it. Her fingers encircled the bars, and the dried blood shifted on her face as she glared. He shifted farther away, to be certain of escaping her farthest reach.

But after a minute, without lunging at him, she said, "Guillaume is a prisoner here. Find him. Make him promise to hide us in the forest if we free him. *Then* we can escape."

"After you enchanted him into prison?" said Roderick.

Her lip curled. "Don't tell him that."


Elisabetta sat back in her seat, and did not care that it was not the royal carriage. It jounced over a stone, and she still did not care.

Then it trundled to a halt. She wondered if another flock of sheep crossed the way.

"Princess?" said the coachman.

She looked out the window. Towers stood, in gold, in rose-red, in green or blue. About them spread blossoming flowerbeds. Those closest to her were filled with purple crocuses and asters. Beside the carriage, an apprentice wizard bowed, his sky blue robes fluttering about him. He sounded breathless when he spoke.

"Your Highness. The wizards wish to speak with you, if it pleases you. They—hope to find the criminals."

Onomastics did not work again, she thought. She reached for the door.

"They can bring the carriage up front, Your Highness," said the apprentice.

"A pleasant walk in a pleasant garden," said Elisabetta. "I have longed for such walks in the last weeks."

Outside, she drew a deep breath of the flowery air. She and the apprentice wound their way around the towers, on paths of chipped white stone. She had barely time to notice the flowers—lilies, snowdrops, roses, asters, daffodils, pinks, tulips—all blooming with cheery disregard for the season—before they arrived at one tower, the only golden one, and taller than all the rest.

There, a door opened on its own, and she walked into a sky-blue chamber. Tables of silver held bowls of crystal and instruments whose clockwork she could not fathom.

"Your Highness!" Wizards bowed to her—two of them, one in robes of black, the other in gray—both robes spangled with stars, suns, and moons.

The gray-robed one, his beard long and white, said, "Your Highness, we wish to show you the nature of our search."

The black-robed one, whose hair and beard were a mix of ginger and gray, spread his hands. "A mysterious matter. Why your father, His Majesty, was Guillaume's godfather! But the onomastics have failed us as if they hid in the Nameless Tower."

"I had men search that before I left the town," she said, dryly.

"That," said the gray-robed one, "is what baffles." He laid his hands on the table. "We wondered whether, during your captivity, you heard anything that might explain—"

She did not think that they breathed. She was not certain she did so herself, not when she remembered Theodore, telling her how she seemed like a cog, slid into place.

"Try this," she said, softly. "Use these names instead: Vicky. Rod. And Will." Beth, she thought, and swallowed that one. She looked from face to face and prayed that they would not ask her why those names.

They bowed.

Clearwater fit its name; the water that flowed between the banks was so clear that she could see the fish even from the shore. Shadowy long brown ones, and goldfish that were white and gold splattered, or fiery red, and as long as her arm.

But then the townsfolk barred her sight, and she nodded and smiled and waved to all the cheering crowds. They could not travel swiftly, between the coachman's care that they could all see their princess's good health, and the excited children in red or flaming orange smocks, who darted across the road this way and that.

At the bridge, the town's officials gathered. She descended from the carriage, and the mayor, in full crimson robes of office, bowed. "Your Highness! Word had been sent to this town but an hour ago, that it might reach you as swiftly as could be."

A murmur ran about the crowd. Elisabetta felt her heart sink. What news could be that urgent? What would she have to do?

"The king's wizards have safely captured your foes! Vittoria, Guillaume, and Roderick are all prisoner, as befits such evildoers!"

Cheers resounded. Before they had died away, the mayor bowed again. "Come within, Your Highness. What better way to celebrate this good news than with a pageant?"

She nodded. "You must have acted swiftly to have it ready to perform."

"Ah, we readied it before then. Days ago, because—" He frowned for a moment. "To celebrate your deliverance. All the more so since our king has no heir but you save for distant cousins."

For a moment, she felt her own face moving toward frowning; she smoothed it out, but she could not forget that, for some reason, she had heard of this festivity before she set out, though every town and half the villages along the way had held them— she had ended half her days hours before sunset to accept such offerings.

In the square before them, a stage stood, its backdrop adorned with golden suns and silver moons. Her eyebrows went up.

"Just as well they started early," said a thin man in charcoal gray robes; the treasurer, she guessed from his seal of offices. "There was trouble because they hadn't cast one role, and some fool had forgotten to give it costume."

"I am certain," said Elisabetta, "that it will prove delightful, nonetheless."

And I will, she vowed, put that strangeness of mind aside for the length of it. Or better yet, for the rest of my journey.

Clockwork birds flew over the royal city, bearing metallic garlands in gold and pink. Elisabetta sat in an open carriage, with all the sky open to her, and even so, had difficulty guessing how many.

The crowd soon made it impossible for her to even try. Banners and garlands, and shouts to the princess—Elisabetta was glad of her seamstress, who had sewed the heavy sky-blue brocade, embroidered with gold, so that she could move freely in it, and the servants who had slipped it out of the castle to her the day before, as she waved and smiled and blew kisses to frolicking children, on the way to the castle. Even the journey here had not inured her to the scale of the celebration.

At the stairs, her parents waited. Even from the bottom, she saw how her father had his arm about her mother, and they clasped their hands. It looked regal, and hid how much it was to hide excitement.

The servants handed her down from the carriage, and she curtseyed, deeply. As royalty, they knew that she had to assure their subjects of her good health, but she had fulfilled that duty. She climbed the stairs. Their eyes gleamed.

"Come in, my dear. These festivities in honor of your safety, and the captivity of those villains, do not suffice. We must hold a feast, as well," said King Baldwin.

Elisabetta smiled back. She suspected the weeks ahead would hold more pageants, feasts, and balls, but a feast would start it properly.

Her father took her right hand, her mother took her left, and in the hall, tables bore plates of gold for the feast. The nobles raised a cheer.

And Theodore emerged. He wore a great, dark cloak and bowed to her smiling father.

"Her Highness," Theodore proclaimed, "won her freedom with a marvelous piece of clockwork. A phoenix. And true to its nature, when the clockwork fell to my hands—"

He drew out from beneath his clock—her phoenix. From his hands, more colorful and well-made than when she had finished, but she could see the form she had labored over.

"A fitting piece of clockwork to celebrate her escape from the Nameless Tower, like a phoenix from the ash."

He threw his hand up. The bird took flight, its wings gleaming in the air, casting gleams of red and orange about the banqueting hall. From all about the hall, she heard indrawn breaths.

Theodore bowed again. "Have no fear, Your Highness. It will be a thousand years before it must burst into flame again!"

Elisabetta laughed. She had not thought of that, but certainly, that had been a wise choice on her part.

# The Lion and the Library

The library, filled with lore and legends and lawsuits, had stout stone walls, thick enough to shield the silence within from any tumult. One could wade through accounts of campaigns against monsters, and chronicles of enchanted gems, without learning of any troubles outside.

Lena, pouring over papers by the light of her sundrop, searching through musty parchments for lions and kings, only slowly realized how long she had done it without Erion's arriving. When it finally dawned on her, she looked about.

From the high windows, the sparse light pierced out, as it did morn or eve or noontide, high overhead; the scholars used sundrops for good reason. Drably clad scholars spoke in low voices, glided among the stacks with sundrops glowing in their hands, or bent over the desks, but they did not include Erion. She knew that, in her bones, before she noted that no one wore a scarf of bright blue, with white stars woven in.

No one else, that was. She fingered her scarf. Erion would have sought her out.

Feeling a cold dread, Lena forced her breath in and out. She could not forfeit the freedom of the library, whatever the news would be. She had proved it useful many times. And—it hurt to think it but—it would be all the more if she became the only one with the freedom, if Erion could not come.

She moved stiffly, gathering up the documents, and swallowed. Erion himself would not approve of her losing it.

Lena blinked against the sunlight. As at dawn so now as well—a bright and cloudless day. The street held fewer people than she had ever seen it, and none were Celestians; she could not see another scarf such as hers for the length of it.

A crowd, full of wailing, surged down the street like waters suddenly freed from a dam. Every one of them wore the scarf. Lena swallowed. The few Solarians on the street eyed the Celestians and for once stepped aside, to avoid this distraught flood. Lena tried to pick out someone, anyone, that she knew, her gaze flitting over them. She did not think there was a woman among them who had her headdress on quite straight.

One woman, despite her reddened eyes, looked, despairingly, at the library. Her mother Mirjam, Lena realized with surprise, and then her mother scrambled up the stairs to her, with no heed for whether anyone went up or down the stairs about her. Her little sister Anila wailed and ran after. Half a dozen other women joined in. Eyes of blue, or violet, looked at her in distress. Lena felt a cold weight lodge in her stomach.

But her mother had her hands. "O my darling, my dove—you must be brave—you must listen—" Tears splattered down her cheek. "Better to hear at once and be done!"

Anila scrambled up beside her, and clung to Lena's arm.

"That evil one, the king's councilor Kudret—he predicted evil days for the king, for King Halis."

Lena felt almost numb. The king. He would do evil of sheer spite if evil befell him. But whatever evil had fallen, they could only suffer and endure; they could do nothing.

Her mother's words inched out. "He went to pick a king out."

Lena felt like ice. She managed to move her mouth. "But not from among the criminals?"

Of course not, came a cool thought. Even in this city, it would take more than a morning to catch Erion and convict him of some crime. Had King Halis chosen such a king, Erion would have joined her, and this crowd would not have formed. . . .

She shuddered. Always before, the kings had gone to avert ill luck by choosing a condemned man to act as king, and take the ill luck, and be executed. She had read the scrolls, heard the tales, exclaimed with the rest beside the hearth—but now it was not some fireside tale. Not when she already knew who had been chosen to suffer at the guards' hands all the days unlucky for the king, and then to be executed at the end.

Her mother babbled on, on how the king had had Kudret summon all the Celestian men, and the women had come to learn the evil news, and Kudret had chosen one. And then could not speak, as if she actually had to reveal the news.

"It's Erion." With great violet eyes, Anila looked solemnly up at her.

Her legs folded under her. She sat on the steps, staring outward, her breath shallow and fast. She had known, she had known, but to hear it was a nightmare. The women fussed about her, and scholars coming out grumbled about the crowd, and both felt like something poking at an unhealed wound. She shuddered.

"Madness," muttered her Aunt Bela, a couple of steps below. "We'll never—I barely managed to wangle the betrothal to him! She'll die unwed for sure."

The slap across her face rang out. Lena, breathing hard, realized that she had stood and glared back at her aunt's bewildered gaze.

"Come." Old Klarita's voice rose from the street, and though she bore a staff, she stood over it like an ancient oak. "We go to King Halis, to reproach him with having set that one, Kudret, to choose his substitute."

Always before the king had chosen a condemned criminal, not from among the Celestians. Nevertheless, as she adjusted her headdress, ensured that her hair was covered by the scarf, Lena felt as barren and bleak as the cold sands of a northern desert that had never known snow. She would go to this court because never again might she have the chance to see Erion.

That thought, sword-like, sliced through her numbness. With half a hundred memories of Erion, from his handing her a nosegay of pale blue spring flowers, to reading together over an ancient scroll of righteous kings, to his standing before her father, solemn, to ask for her hand in marriage.

Tears welled up in her eyes. The shifting crowd bore her along.


Celestians gathered like birds descending after winter, though their whispers were softer than the birds' twittering. Here, even more pitying glances fell on her. She felt too fraught with bitter pain to care. Erion, Erion—she would not care to marry if he died—

If? She let her mother and sister bundle her forward—the crowd parted for them—and only wallowed in her folly. If! As if King Halis would regard it as anything but a fate a Celestian had earned!

They stopped. She realized that they had brought her to below the dais, where she could see all, and be seen. Just where, perhaps, his parents might have stood if Erion had not been an orphan— Her mother took one of her hands. Anila took the other. And King Halis appeared on the balcony, beneath the roof that shadowed his royal scarlet until it looked not like fresh blood, but dark blood from a mortal wound.

A murmur came through the crowd. Lena saw the guards in dark armor and got a glimpse, but only a glimpse, of the gold and royal scarlet before she docilely bowed her head with the rest.

When she raised it again, the crowd had parted, far more readily than it had for her. The first guards still lashed out with their staffs, inflicting bruises and blood on the pretense of

clearing the way. In the center of the clump, Erion walked, in
gold and scarlet robes, and in chains. His face was grave and set,
and he did not glance to either side. His lip showed blood, and
the side of his face, a bruise. He did not falter, but a guard still
shoved him onward. She could not see all the gemstones they
bore on wristbands or sword hilts, but she saw enough tiger's
eyes. Erion could not flee past their sight.

Anila squeaked. Lena looked down. Her knuckles had grown
white with her grip. She loosened her fingers—it felt like freeing
manacles that had held for centuries—and forced her breath in
and out. They could not misuse him too badly, or he would not
live to suffer execution, only at the end of the unlucky days.

In the shadows of the Queen's Niche, something moved.
Lena blinked. That foreign princess Pulcherie sprawled there, a
pale shadow, and her attendants hovered about her like birds
about a new hatchling, and Lena hated her.

A light pattering of feet drew her eyes aside again. An old
man, lean like a cricket, his hair paler than sunlit clouds, wore not
the blue scarfs that others did, but a robe with stars and the
moon woven in. He ran down the cleared path. Though the
guards had already hauled Erion before the balcony, the crowd
murmured and stayed back for him.

"Petrit," said Lena.

"The hermit?" said Anila, sharply. Their mother hushed her,
but Lena kept her eyes on Petrit. It would indeed take a miracle
to aid them. Petrit did not glance aside and stopped only at the
dais. The king, his eyes narrowed, studied him.

"A terrible fate awaits you, o king!" Petrit's voice rang from
the building, and her stomach roiled. Encourage King Halis to
think of his own danger? Erion looked away, as if regally
dismissing the hermit from his thoughts, and stood with his face
set like flint.

"A dreadful fate will befall you on those days—you will
become a murderer!"

Petrit swept his hand toward the sky. "It is the fate of men under the sun to suffer illness and accident, but no man is forced to shed innocent blood. That is the fate you may yet avoid."

King Halis's lip curled. "This is no time for a mountebank to try to amuse me." His hand moved downward through the air like a headsman's axe. The guards headed toward Petrit.

"To add to your sins to silence them—is to pile folly on folly," said Petrit, and to Lena's relief, drew back so quickly that the guards stayed to guard the king.

The king surveyed the crowd.

Zenil stepped forward and bowed. He had prospered as a merchant, but his clothing showed only a touch of his wealth in the fineness of the cloth. His face showed even less fear.

"Your Majesty," he said, his voice deep and grave, "you astound me. Alas, the prisons burst with those deserving of death, and yet you must choose a man guilty of no crime?"

"How," said King Halis, sounding almost as grave, "could I inflict such a king on my people?"

Zenil's face spasmed, but a moment later, unable to say that the pretended king would have no power, he said, "For your sake, Your Majesty, we could endure it."

King Halis hesitated.

"Do not do it," said Kudret, smoothly, at the king's elbow. "Do not even consider it. How, Your Majesty, is suffering a just execution *misfortune*? The one who must take your place must suffer those days' misfortune." He shook his head. "There are kings who foolishly chose murderers to take their place, and the ill luck was not averted."

Because it is a foolish superstition, thought Lena. Both the foretelling and the foolish attempt to avert it.

Kudret's voice rolled smoothly on. "A king must consider how his fate affects his kingdom."

King Halis nodded.

"Besides—a Celestian! He insults the Unconquerable Sun!" Kudret swept a hand toward Erion. "Look at him. Even his own eyes warn him that he should have turned aside from his ways!"

His tone grew warmer, and his words more swift. "Why, it would be better for him to suffer death to save Your Majesty, than if the Sun withheld the mercy he has extended so long, and completed what he began, by turning the knave into a bird, or a fish, or a cat, as he has already begun by giving him their eyes." Kudret drew a deep breath. "But then, who can understate their folly, who see daily the radiance of the Unconquerable Sun, and yet deny it for some—thing that can not be seen?"

"How true," said King Halis, coldly.

"But, Your Majesty," said old Vidrum, a silver-haired scribe limping forward, "how can you speak so heartlessly before his very betrothed?"

Every gaze followed his gesture toward her, and she hoped she looked lovely and anguished—before she doubted. Would he have been less monstrous to have chosen among the widowed or the unbetrothed? He would just choose another, if he heeded Vidrum's appeal.

King Halis looked troubled. Her heart leapt, for all her doubts.

A sigh came out of the Queen's Niche, heard only in the silence. "O my heart, o the soul of my life." Even for this, Queen Pulcherie's voice sounded languid. "O, do not risk yourself, do not imperil yourself, do not endanger yourself—I can not bear it, think of my love and do not harm my heart—"

King Halis twitched, like a horse throwing off a fly.

"Enough of these appeals. This wretch has been called to an honor far beyond his desert. He shall do his duty. Whoever seeks to stay me shall not see him perish, for he shall die first!"

He looked at Erion, and got Erion's steady gaze back. He flinched, but—he would not change his will.

Abed, Lena studied the ceiling's whitewash. Her arms sprawled on the mattress, her face felt slack, and nothing stirred any desire to move in her. Grayish sunlight seeped into the room. She closed her eyes. No one would rouse her if she did not stir.

No one would venture to the library to find anything that might aid Erion, as she and Erion had found that water stone, if she did not stir.

And if no sober history would tell of such aid, neither had any such history told of the water stone.

There was still the lion and its heart. For a moment, her mouth twisted. Perhaps the king had lied, and Erion had been chosen for his knowledge of it. She doubted it. The king's minsters and the king himself did not think highly of the scholars, to listen to them, and the scholars did not think of highly of Erion, to learn what he searched for. She, and she alone, knew.

Lena sighed. Then she swung her legs off the bed and pushed herself up to stand, blinking like an owlet, with her shift falling to her ankles. She would hate the library. There was not a shelf there that would not remind her of Erion.

Dress first, she thought, and found every step of it required thought to move her hands through it. Over her shift, her smock. Her overdress, and to lace that up—it took concentration to tighten up the ribbons, and five times as long as she needed with her wits about her. Her coat. Her mantle. Sit on the bed to don stocking and shoe. Up again to brush out her hair and be glad they could afford no such frivolity as a mirror. She reached for her headdress.

As she adjusted the combs to hold it on, Anila started at the door.

"Oh, you're up."

Lena pushed the comb firmly in place. "It is the king who is Erion's misfortune. He will not hear that my grief slew me even before his own death."

Anila blinked.

Lena headed out, and down the narrow stair to the kitchen. Porridge. Though her betrothed lay under sentence of death, some of her gloom was hunger.

Her mother looked up from the porridge pot. "You look ready for the street."

"I am going to the library. To look—"

Aunt Bela hooted. "Library? What help is the library? No law will protect us, and were there twenty—a hundred—laws and more, the king would ignore them all."

She rambled on, and Lena passed her to take the bowl her mother gave her. If she had held her tongue, she might not have had to suffer until her escape to the street.

Bela threw her hands into the air. "It's utterly useless!"

Lena ate, did not lift her gaze from the bowl, and was glad she had not told all. Bela would jeer all the more if she had said she did not go to piece together futile law, but legend.

She, and Erion, had found the water stone that way. She stood and laid aside the bowl. For a moment, she stared down at her hands, still on it, and remembered the transparent stone, the lightest of greens, and how it had for a moment glinted among the dark rounded rocks of the dry spring, before water had come to cover all, and make all glint.

She pulled her hands away. Her family had paid the dowry of four daughters out of the money for that. But now she wanted something greater than that.

In the cloudy day, the street held as many people as ever, scurrying about, wearing the blue scarf by law, but though they went about their business, they seemed subdued. Even the haggling went on in low voices, and most of it seemed to be for food. Insults to each other's ancestors or diet did not resounded the length of the street at all, let alone every few minutes. No one stopped on a corner to talk. Even the women waiting to draw water did not chatter among themselves.

Lena scurried with the rest, down narrow streets, still overshadowed by the dingy buildings, neither gray nor brown, that lined the street. Bela had had this much right: Erion had not found a clear document, but one he had asked her to look at as well. To be sure, he had not thought the Lion's Heart a certainty to be more than a curious legend. But any magic that could defend the innocent—what other hope did she have? And the danger to her was not terrible. If she failed, she might escape all notice, and only Erion would suffer.

Anguish nearly doubled her over. She fought to steady her breath. How Bela would scold her—such unseemly devotion for her to feel before the marriage ceremony. Even her mother would gravely disapprove. She forced her breath out. She should have, she told herself, seek this legend out whomever Kudret had chosen.

Though Erion's aid would have made it easier, had the choice fallen on any other.

She fled down the street over the cobblestones as if she could outrun the pain.

Three corners later, she reached a street more busy, with fewer of the blue scarfs. She slowed before she collided and caused offense. Her breath came as harshly as if wolves had chased her over a mountainside. Some passersby glanced at her, perhaps in recognition, perhaps just noting the scarf and the Celestian, whose disfavor at law they had recently been reminded of. She forced her breath to ease. Stealth and silence would be needed allies if she were to succeed at all.

A church along the way gleamed with gold and candlelight, as brilliant as the sun on a clear day. Songs resounded, sonorously. Lena crept to the other side alongside, unable to close her ears to the prayers of petition for the king's wellbeing and the triumph of averting evil from him.

Lena did not even look over.


She had to put her sundrop down on the shelf to keep the light from trembling over the scrolls like sunlight through wind-shaken leaves. She smoothed out the parchment with double care. Erion had not been foolish to ask her to look at it again. If he had not spoken of it, she would have wondered whether the scrolls had really talked of the lions of legend in their poetic lines about perfection and rubies.

And justice. Above all else, the legends spoke of justice. But first she had to deal with perfection and ruby, and at that, she could only pray that a teeming royal city did not hold two perfect rubies of that size.

In spite of herself, her mouth twitched. Or perhaps that the Master of Heavens would guide her steps to the right one, no matter how many the city held.

Her gaze drifted over the room, the shadows, the motes of light in a sunbeam, the shelves and shelves and shelves of books. Her breath came out as she remembered standing here, and Erion speaking to her. Grave, composed, as if he had feared that anything less dignified would inspire her to take him for a fool, telling her they could find the way, into the treasury, by routes the Solarians would fear to tread. In these books.

She did not need to read them all. She had even read, before, many ones that she wanted now. Then she had laid them aside because venturing to the tunnels had been rash and useless.

It was not yet useful. Her teeth worried her lower lip. She had time. Indeed, she had to take her time, to await the hour of Erion's coronation, before she struck.

Still, she rolled up the scroll, to go and claim another. Using the days and hours to take care would be wiser, especially as she had to commit her route to memory. She walked among the soft-voiced scholars and among the shelves. This route she had already mastered.

A soft cough sounded. At the end of those shelves, Rodvan stood. Another man stood by him—dark as Rodvan was, with features alike as well, and young, perhaps younger than she was. She looked back, her eyes narrowed, and her hand lingered on the scroll.

He's just, said a sly thought. He knows your great grief. He won't hold it against you.

She sighed, and her shoulders slumped. She almost wished, as she came forward, that she could ask him for aid, but for all his graciousness to her and to Erion, Rodvan remained a Solarian.

And probably could do nothing for either of them, at that.

"I rejoice to see you in good health," said Rodvan, his voice formal, his deer-dark eyes solemn. "My son has returned from abroad in good health, and bearing books that perhaps will interest you."

Lena bowed her head and murmured politeness on his return.

"They talk of allowing only Solarians to view them."

For a moment, Lena could not breathe. Such blind pettiness, to corner her to tell her that—she would never have dreamed—

"My daughter—" His voice was very heavy. "—you should consider your folly. Surely even you have suffered to see the imprudence—"

"I—" Her voice was as harsh as a crow's, but it silenced him. She swallowed. "I can not foreswear the Master of Heaven and Earth, to whom I owe my being, and who has set my feet on this path."

Rodvan said, "The Sun is the source of all being—it can plainly be seen—even the stars and the moon are but its shadows—how could a being that can not even be seen have more power than the Glorious Sun?"

Her face set.

A moment after, with a nod of his head, he stepped aside. His son bowed and went with him. Tunnels, Lena reminded herself, with a bitter taste in her mouth, and the sour thought that Rodvan spoke out of nothing but kindness.

She still had to go in the same direction that Rodvan had gone. She walked with all the dignity she could muster, and the son, in a voice almost low enough that she could not hear, told his father that he should wait until her great grief had receded.

Feeling cold, hollow, and alone, she turned down one row, not even able to feel glad that she followed them no longer. Perhaps her aunt Bela would be pleased, though Rodvan would not, of course, venture to propose a betrothal so soon, or even once Erion was decently dead but not long in his grave.

And he would never, of course, even think of his son's becoming a Celestian to wed her, however otherwise fit she was as a bride.

She slept restlessly that night; every time she drifted into slumber, dreams of rubies—rubies larger than her joined fists, dark as garnets or heart's blood, looming in darkness—woke her again, leaving her panting and horrified past reason. Once, she leaned back against her pillow and wondered if the dreams bore warnings. She stared out into the unanswering darkness.

Across the room, Anila shifted and sighed. At least, her sister slept like a log, and she would not have to explain why she slept so restlessly. . . .

Though she would not have. Anila would think them dreams of Erion, and ask no questions.

Lena could feel the bitterness in her smile. And then memory slid to Erion with an ancient scroll in hand, pointing her to how a perfect ruby would not only glow of its own, like a coal, but how it could work magic.

Anila, perched on the hearth with her mending, looked brightly up at Lena. "It can't be that hard, Lena. You and Erion both looked on your own in less than a year." She waved a hand in the air. "You had to ask questions after, but don't all of the scholars have to ask *sometimes*?"

Lena forced her breath in and out. Behind her, their mother moved about with the clean breakfast dishes. She said nothing, though she must have heard Anila's talk, and her question. Likely, she thought that training Anila would distract Lena nicely, even at the risk of having a second bookish daughter.

Lena swallowed. Her mother would be no help, but she still had to refuse. Hard enough that Rodvan might spy what she did. Anila would be all over it in moments if she were in the library.

"It's work," she said. "Hard work. It takes much searching to find anything useful."

"Like the waterstone. That must have been wonderful to watch, but I didn't get to see it."

Lena remembered. The stone, clear as air, pale green, flashing in Erion's hand as he threw it down among the dry stones—the water that rose as smoothly as a mist—the next morning, when she had roused from her sleep in the shepherds' hut to see the streamside covered with flowers like blue stars, and the oldest shepherds declaring that they had indeed seen such blossoms, when they were children—and she could only hope that she had not exhausted her ability to find marvels. She still had the crown of flowers that Erion had woven for her, but it was so dried that the colors were little more than memories.

Anila tugged her sleeve, to grab her attention. "And if I worked anywhere else," she said triumphantly, "I'd work just as hard, and never even have a chance to see such a thing."

Lena's mouth tightened. "I haven't—I can't train you quickly enough."

"There is that," said their mother, quietly, from the doorway. Lena glanced over, and flinched. Before her stood Solok and Klarita, and they had not only arrived uncommonly early to visit and gossip, but both women eyed her as avidly as a beggar would a feast.

"But," her mother continued, "you would have to start some time. It is best to keep busy in evil times." Her mouth curved, though nothing else in her face smiled.

"Oh yes oh yes," murmured Solok and Klarita together, their heads bobbing up and down like leaves buffeted by a wind as they edged into the room. Lena, wary, circled around them.

"It's so dreadful," said Solok. "Parading him about like the king had actually chosen his heir. So ghastly."

"And the bruises!" said Klarita. "You'd think the guards were trying to beat him to death before the day." She shuddered. "*So* dreadful."

"I have to go now," said Lena. "The sooner I finish the tasks I have to do alone, the sooner I can train Anila." Her hand reached for the doorframe, and she forced it down and into a fist before she could try to steady herself before those two ghouls. Her mother looked severe, and she fled.

Behind her, their voices rose again, shrilly discussing how much harder it would be for Lena alone, perhaps she should not venture to such hard duties. . . .

Beneath the cloudy sky, in the chilly air, she hurried. She had no need to go to the library. To read every scroll and codex a seventh time would not make them yield up new secrets, and hunting about for more would reap little. She had preparations to make, but putting them off until the last minute would mean she had less time to hide them. Perhaps she could have taught Anila in the meantime.

A blast of wind gusted down the street, pulling at her skirt.

She had given her excuse already, and it would be unwise to undermine it. And she might find more knowledge, and she doubted she could keep herself from searching. And the farther Anila was from her work, the better—if only to keep her from betraying her, or being stained by her deeds.

Thunder grumbled, far off in the distance, and she let out her breath. She should look for other knowledge. Another thing like the waterstone would aid even if her plan utterly failed, and Erion died.

A raindrop splattered against the cobblestones, leaving a trace larger than many coins. Lena hurried up the stairs toward the door, not so quickly as to avoid the rainfall that speckled the street like a leopard's skin, but she stepped within before it did more than splatter. She hurried deeper inside, and the rain hurled itself against the roof, so heavily that single drops could not be made out in the clatter.

She had good reason not to return any time soon.

She glanced up. Despite decades of grime, on the ceiling, the lapis lazuli blue with its gilt sun, the black with silver moon and stars, glinted to remind her that the library had once been a Celestian church. She let her breath out. The Master of Heavens could still guide her steps here.

Those scholars who moved about the vast room did so as gravely as ever, but far fewer of them than usual, and so the light was more dim, with so few sundrops. Lena moved across the floor, as silently as she could, as always.

Down one bookcase, Rodvan inspected a scroll. Then his gaze caught hers, and he jumped and shoved it away. Lena stood still a moment. Without his movement, she would never have noted where he stood, at what he looked, but that scroll had been among those she had looked at.

And gawking like this had told him that she had guessed that. She turned her face away and walked on, as the rain resounded, overhead. She could hope that he would not guess before she could strike, or even that his fondness for a bright young scholar would dissuade him from acting against her.

She found the shelf she sought, but she had to draw a breath to steady herself before she took up a codex. Despite everything, she would be glad when Erion's mockery of a coronation was over. She could do so little before then.

Though not nothing.

In the gloomy vault, her heart pattered. She hurried over the floor's flagstones.

When desecrating the church, the Solarians had kept no records of it. If she had not visited the books that an old Celestian scholar had kept privately, she would never have known what was stored down here, and how it was guarded.

Which meant good hope of finding it still there.

The jug of water sweated in her hands, and left a trail of dark splatters behind her. Her fingers tightened on its neck, though they had started to numb. She had drawn it straight from a spring for its bone-chilling cold, and now—her gaze darted about. She could see if it could not—

A soft hiss resounded. Lena glanced about again. The scales were brown and barely caught the light, but the snake glided over the stone. Its blind head turned to and fro as it sought out the heat that had roused it.

Lena put one hand to the jug bottom to hold it more firmly. The snake slithered closer. She tilted the jug and flung the water, spraying both snake and stone. The guardian recoiled from the chill, and Lena ran past it, deeper into the vaults, clutching the jug to her as if it were a child.

With the snake behind her, she slowed. Even after she caught her breath, her heart hammered, but she did not stop. The light shone no more brightly than starlight would, but she could picked her way. Her mouth twitched. She held out the jug again, away from her, though the water in it sloshed. Her clothes were already wet. She could only hope that it would dry after she found her way down, and back.

"Commend your cares and whatever troubles your heart," she whispered, "to the trusty hands of Him Who set the stars. He who set the heavens in order and appointed their hours will also find paths where your feet can walk."

After a moment, she smiled. Of course the water had worked. The snake was the guardian of a treasury, where they wished to go in and out if they needed the treasures; they needed some way to stop its poison; it could not be too difficult.

The doorway loomed before her. It was not much larger than she was, but even against this gloom, it seemed dark. Carefully, Lena set down the jug—it took a moment to steady it on the rough floor —and, looking away, drew out the sundrop.

It still blinded as light flooded the vault and cast her enormous shadow against the stones.

Lena blinked. Moments later, she held the stone to one side and picked her way into the secret chamber. Even through her watering eyes, she made out glints here and there—treasures that a conqueror could have had, if only he had been less bloodthirsty, or had not treated scholars as less than dead leaves blown by the wind.

She looked past them. Gold and jewels would not buy Erion's life. She dashed her hand over her eyes, and a silvery gleam caught her gaze, long enough for her to make out the rope. Her breath stole out. Gold and jewels could last long, down in this snake-guarded labyrinth, but only enchantment could preserve a rope of spider silk. To still be here showed that it was what the parchments had said.

Lena slipped closer, realizing she felt more fearful than delighted, but nonetheless, she reached out. Her fingers closed on the rope. Though smoother than any rope she had ever touched before—and most thread—it felt solid, and lifting it from the shelf meant only that flopped down from her hand, not that it crumbled into dust.

"You read too many legends," she charged herself.

The echoes died about her. A hiss sounded from the doorway.

For a moment, she felt as if she had plunged head first into the spring herself. She whipped about. The snake lifted its blind head to lick the air and hiss again. Even as her mouth went dry, it slithered past the jug.

Too far, too far, she thought, stumbling backward. The vault did not hold enough room for her to be sure of running about it—her waist struck one shelf—even were the snake not heading toward her like a slow but well-aimed arrow.

The rope fell from her fingers, and her hand fumbled back and closed about something like a handle. Blindly, she threw it.

The knife pierced its head. For a moment, it strained against it, and its coils thrashed about as the blood bubbled. Not red blood. Blacker than starless midnight. Lena fought down her panic, but the snake had fallen still before she had mastered it. Still breathing light and fast, she crouched to take up the rope and sling it over her shoulder before she inched toward the door.

The knife handle, she thought, looked like bone. She swallowed a laugh for fear of what would follow, and a stray thought idly said, "He will find paths where your feet can walk."

She stood a minute longer. This was the treasury. What it contained was well worth the protections of the vault. No one would be fool enough to place a commonplace knife here.

Picking her way about the dead coils and the black pool of blood, telling herself that she did so for fear of betraying bloodstains, she found a stretch of stone close enough to reach.

The knife came free too easily, considering the skull it must have struck. Though it bore blood on the blade, it did not drip.

She scampered for the doorway. There, not knowing whether there were more snakes, she slid away the sundrop. The gloom returned.

Moments later, her eyes seeing as much as they could, she bent to take up the jug and lugged it along as she crept through the labyrinth again.

When the light had increased again, even past what the stone could shed, Lena braced herself and looked at the knife again. The blood, still damp, looked not black but deep purple.

She winced and put down the jug to wash the blade with the last of the water. The rope she would hide here until the hour to strike. The knife—the knife she would carry with her. It was small enough to hide.


A strange hum, like a vast beehive, filled the city on the eve of the coronation. Even among the Solarians, it did not sound only of excitement. Still, she had to walk among them, on her way.

Her stomach felt like a mob of butterflies. Wherever she went, silence and gazes followed her, followed by sibilant whispers. She tried to walk calmly, as if she were nothing more than she had been, but while the words did not carry, the fascination in them did. As if Erion's first decree would be to summon her and make her his queen, and partaker of his fate. As if the coronation would grant Erion the power to make decrees.

She looked up at the library.

"You fool! Courting your doom!"

A hermit pressed through the crowd—dirtier and more ragged than Petrit—aimed utterly at her. Every passerby shifted from his path; some looked at him with fear; he ignored every one of them.

"You, venturing there still? After what befall Erion? It was no more than the justice." He threw his hands in the air. "To walk on the floors dedicated to the Most High, to the Master of Heavens, as if it were meant to house mere parchments!"

Lena flinched back. I need—I aid Celestians—but she kept her tongue. To encourage him would be worse folly. She looked about for a clear way. She saw no signs of guards, and flinched away from that thought. Even this madman did not deserve what the guards would do if they caught him.

"Do not tell me that we profit from your *scholarship*!"

Her heart seemed to stop, and then to hammer.

"Let the Solarians store up the wrath of the Master of Heavens for paltry coins! To go freely is to accept the desecration!"

She ran. Master of Heavens guide her, she ran with no heed to her footing, down streets—startling a flight of doves and drawing stares—around corners and over-laden donkeys, up stairs—at the height, the square held a fountain, plashing away, and Lena forced herself to stop. Her breath came harshly. A low wall blocked off the fall, and she leaned on it to steady herself. Vendors and passersby slowly stopped staring at her. Tales would probably spread about how Erion's bride had gone mad and run wild.

But not that she had gone into the library that had been a church. How could going there tell anyone anything when no one remembered it had been a church?

Three doves came slowly circling down. The first one, a shade of grayish brown that matched the stones, settled on the flagstones. Lena sighed. The other two followed. The brown of their breast was almost rosy.

If the Master of Heavens entrusted something small to you, such as entrance to the library, it was wise to use it wisely, lest he never entrust anything greater. She stood, straightened her head dress, and started down the stairs.

"Isn't her age enough?" Bela's sharp voice came through the kitchen door. Lena, uncommonly weary, hesitated in the shadowed street, though the moon already showed pale against the darkening sky, and the kitchen fire illuminated only a scrap of the flagstones. "Her oddities? The way she has always dressed like a widow just past mourning?"

Lena's mouth twitched. No one would hire a scholar not soberly dressed.

"Does she have to run down the city streets like a madwoman?"

Mirjam's voice was measured and dry. "Her great grief has turned her wits. We can easily explain her failure to wed, thus." A soft clatter spoke of her scraping some ingredient into a dish. "She can live with a sister, and her nieces will no doubt find her a figure from a ballad and even think that the king executed Erion out of jealousy."

Lena's mouth twisted. If ever a man was worth going mad for, it was Erion. She walked forward and softly announced her return.

Anila looked up from the pot on the hearth.

"Soup's near ready," she caroled.

"We shall have to eat well," said Lena. "The ceremony will be long, we will need our strength."

Because we will stand every moment of it. With the sky lowering lead gray over them, like the pall over a coffin.

Whoever was nearest her had murmured and looked at her. Some had urged her closer, as if the sight of a commonplace Celestian woman, like any other, would touch the king's heart— or as if she craved the sight of Erion's coronation.

She fingered her scarf. Between the dark buildings, every inch of cobblestone held the crowd, Solarian and Celestian. More Celestians, she thought, though who could judge with everyone on the level? A few bold souls leaned out of the lowest windows, but on some walls, even they risked being higher than the king.

Great bellowing cries of Henya! drew her gaze like a lodestone to the balcony. A crier, extravagant in violet and gold, proclaimed the great misfortune of the loss of King Halis, to be lamented by all below the sun—King Halis the brave, the wise, the prudent, the just, the temperate, the merciful, the generous, the magnanimous—

The crowd stood even more still and silent than usual for such a proclamation. Lena could not have sworn that she heard anyone breathe. A hawk's shrill cry, from where it circled, too high to be seen clearly, still resounded over them as if over a mountain valley where not even a flock of sheep grazed.

"Hence, a new king shall reign! May King Erion's virtues be as great as his predecessors!"

That, thought Lena, would not be difficult.

"And his reign as long and glorious!"

Lena shivered and pulled her mantle closer. She got only a glimpse of Erion as they hauled him forward, and forced herself to straighten. His robes were scarlet, heavily embroidered with gold, making his face look all the paler above them. Unbruised, Lena thought, and felt relief that she knew was madness. They had known what his coronation robes could not cover, and she could not know what injuries the robes could.

Bela whispered. "They got new robes to give King Halis, when he's crowned again. *Those* are cloth-of-gold."

Lena flinched.

At least Erion moved easily, she told herself. Servants moved about to disrobe him, down to the long white shirt—even on this cloudy day, it looked as bright as a wisp of cloud before the sun. The pallor of his hands and face blended insensibly with it.

And with him clad in this light attire, a hierophant in heavy white robes solemnly began the injunctions to rule wisely and well, and the duties of the righteous king, on and on and on, as if the abdication had slackened Halis's authority in the slightest. Even with Halis ensconced in the evening house—an old name for a tomb, and fitting for the palace where he would wait out this.

Wind blew over them. Lena shivered and wondered whether Erion was cold.

The invocation went on, but servants lifted the robes, to clad him in majesty.

They presented him with a sword, to deliver justice.

They crowned him with gold and ruby, to indicate rule.

They led him before the balcony, and called on the crowd to hail him as king.

Lena shouted with the rest and only after wondered how this false coronation could stir such a shout. Doves, startled, leapt from their perches and whirled through the air in great flocks. When the shout dwindled, their frantic coos echoed in its wake.

Aunt Bela's lip curled as she watched the flock. "Supposed to be a good sign, that. Supposed to mean a reign of peace."

Her voice was pitched so low that Anila looked up her, baffled. Lena swallowed, turned from the sky, and stared at Erion, knowing she might never see him again. Very likely that all his reign would know no war.

The crowd moved hesitantly at first, like ice half-clogging a spring river, but then they dispersed into the streets and alleyways. Lena almost wished she had worn an overmantle; to be thought overly pious and modest, hiding her face in shadow, would nonetheless be better than the pitying glances.

The sight of blue beside her made her blink and turn. Petrit looked gravely at her. Lena opened her mouth and shut it again.

"Do not despair, my daughter," he said. "Those who die do not depart from us forever. They go before us on a journey, which we must one day follow, as all men must."

Lena looked at him for a long minute, having no notion what she could say. Then, mutely, she bowed her head. He raised his hand to bless her.

Surely, she needed every blessing she could get.

"Better to have gone around," muttered Bela at the next stairs, where the swarm of people clumped again, waiting to descend.

Anila's nose wrinkled. "Like a donkey?"

"A donkey would be smarter than us, to forgo these stairs," said Mirjam. "It would be swifter, even if it would take us farther." She did not, however, shift from where she stood in the crowd.

Lena, abruptly feeling as if she could not breathe, broke free, out of the herd, to the empty flagstones past the crowd. Down the street ahead of her, people already vanished into their homes or their shops, free from the coronation and about their lives, leaving her all but alone on the stones. She drew in a deep breath.

"There she is!"

The voice boomed from high up; two stairs—both filled with people—stood between her and the soldiers staring down. Still, one pointed at her. They started to shove through the crowds, tossing people aside and ignoring cries of pain.

Lena ran.

Before she past three streets, this level opened out, and she darted down alleyways to hide. After two quick turns, she slowed, before the strange fleeing woman could draw the guards' gaze. Even after her breath grew less ragged, her heart still hammered. Perhaps it would be Erion who followed her on that journey—

If they were wise to her, now that Erion was crowned, she had every reason to act and none to wait. She had even carried the dagger with her—and perhaps they had learned from Erion what he and she had looked for in the library.

A hawk screamed, far overhead. She wondered whether it had struck down any of the doves in flight, and walked toward the library. Her heart calmed, but she felt colder than well water as she walked.

Guards, bristling with weapons, loomed on the library stairs—as many of them as if they protected the king. They went in and out freely, shocking Lena despite herself. Scholars puffed up like bantam cocks in indignation, and deflated again when they faced the captain, who had not drawn a sword, but who lowered over the stairs as if he would strike dead with a glance anyone ventured in.

As if the stairs were its only entrance, she told herself.

Wishing she had slipped off her blue scarf in the alleyway, half-glad that she had not thought of it and so did not face the strange prospect of walking down the street without it, she joined the flow of walkers streaming by. Her half-suppressed glances at the library did not mark her out among the others as she slowly circled about the building.

Every time she faced a new doorway, even one that was half-buried in the earth, with a stairway leading down, guards stood ready to seize intruder. As if they knew of the rope, and deemed it wiser to keep her from it than to capture her.

Her stomach felt like a cold weight as she let herself go on, and avoid the guards' gazes. Gawking was one thing—the crowds filled the street to do it—but the guards would fall upon whomever came close.

She had not sought out the rope for nothing, but it would not help her now.

Her hand crept toward the dagger. Then she forced it away. The guards were more guilty than a mindless snake, but even one guard might prove more than she could overpower—certainly, whatever the powers of the knife, he might cry for aid before she killed him—and the captain had never been fool enough to set only one.

She could think of a thousand things where she might need that rope. And she could think of a thousand more things that she might need for this. Trying with only the dagger and the sundrop was only a little more foolish than if she had rope as well. The folly lay in trying at all.

She walked off, more briskly, startling those about her and drawing angry demands that she watch where she went.


She would not have guessed that she would need as much time as she did to find the stair and the grotto.

Guards moved along the street and scowled at every passer-by. Though she did not know how she managed it, she flinched no more than an honest subject would, and they did not pick her out, even to give her a second look. Indeed, the rest of the crowd seemed to notice her no more than—she let her breath out as the thought struck—than before coronation.

Guards descended to the tunnels by ways she would never had chosen, until she wondered how so many could search when they had to guard two kings. Neither the guards nor the crowds hampered her as she wove her way through the labyrinth of buildings as gray as the clouds.

Finally, she reached the tiny square. A tabby cat darted off, across the cobblestones, and left her alone there.

Lena did not linger. She might not be alone for long. Her heartbeat hammered in her ears as she strode over, between two gargoyles, and down narrow stairs into air smelling of dusk and damp and stone. She had ventured here once, and for her own childish whim, when first she had read of it. She could venture farther for good cause. Her mouth twisted. As the king's only loyal subject, one could say it was her duty to venture farther.

"So. You did." The voice, echoing faintly from the stone, was hollow and despairing.

Lena froze as if turned to stone. Long moments later, she realized that she knew the voice, for all the strangeness of its tone. She turned. The gloom did not hide Rodvan's pale face.

It had, after all, been Rodvan who had shown her the tome that spoke of this tunnel. She swallowed. He could easily have worked out what maps she had consulted, to find a map of them all.

"I guessed." His voice was soft. "If you were truly bent on madness as the guards said you were, you would come here." He took a step forward. "My child, is not one of you enough? Erion did not imprudently throw his life away, at that."

Lena braced herself. She glanced by him. The doorway downward loomed to Rodvan's right.

Rodvan's words sped more swiftly. "I can conceal your odd behavior. Whatever any fool says, I can claim to know better, and explain more. But you must come with me, at once. To go down in the tunnels—the guards will never believe." He stepped forward, and spread an imploring hand. "If you are so lucky as to fall in their hands. Your path will take you into the underground, forsaken of the Glorious Sun. They are unblessed and the haunts of monsters."

"The Master of Heavens can guide my path," said Lena. "Wherever I go."

"My child—"

She drew the dagger.

He blinked and drew back.

"Now you may tell the guards that I forced you to let me." She closed her mouth before she babbled. Her heartbeat pulsed so loudly she thought she would not hear anything he said.

She did not dare turn her back on him; Rodvan might yet risk the dagger to save her. But sidling by him, swiftly, while his shocked face was still bent on the knife, brought her to the door. She hurtled down the way, not minding the shadows, trusting in her childhood memory, and listened. Her own footsteps echoed from the stones, but none others following.

As the floor leveled out, she stopped. Her breath sounded hoarse in her ears. Once it had calmed, her heartbeat drummed. The doorway showed in the gloom as a gleam of light, with no shadow falling from it. She turned her face away. Even the dim entrance would blind her, here, where neither sunlight nor moonlight nor starlight ever struck.

Other lights did, and moments later, her eyes adjusted, Lena recognized the gleam. Her breath caught. Sundrops. But even with swords and spears ready, the soldiers could not have prodded the scholars into a search; they would fuss and fuss and then search ineffectually.

Her heart started to hammer again.

Which meant that the guards knew the tunnels, with the briskness that they moved. Whatever they may have feared about venturing underground, to where the sunlight never reached.

She pulled her headdress forward, to muffle her face, and picked her way onward. The glints made finding her footing possible if difficult. Her own stone was near enough to hand to catch, if she needed to run.

The light reflected oddly, and footsteps resounded down stones. No one approached. Then, they could not tell she walked down there—

She started, and her eyes shut in a moment of frustration. And they would not tell that even by her light, since they had stolen the scholars'. For her to walk with it might even send them off on other ways, thinking that another soldier searched there, where footsteps without light would draw them to find the intruder.

She drew out her sundrop. Light gleamed redly through her fingers until she turned up her hand. It glowed. Even in these dingy, ancient tunnels of stone and brick, and grime, the light was as golden as ripened wheat.

The shadows it cast, from pillars, and through arched doorways, were darker than night. She picked out her way onward, hurrying as best she could. And always, off in the distance, lights glinted, and footsteps resounded.

She had yet to even reach a third of the way. One came so close she could almost make out the guard himself; she bit her lip and ducked into a niche as if searching it. A minute later, her heart pattering, she emerged. He had gone on. She might yet lose them, Lena told herself; she was not searching as they were, and could travel more swiftly. Occasionally, shouts resounded. For a moment, she fancied that her light footfall would betray her to the clomping soldiers.

Then a muffled sound, like the footfalls of a ghost, absorbed her attention entirely.

For a moment, her gaze darted about, seeking the noise in the shadows. Her hand trembled, and a thousand movements encircled her. She picked out nothing until the padding of footfalls returned. Then, light glinted from first an eye and then from a pale, pale face, surrounded by locks as white as lichen, and far too high above the floor. Vaguely, still in the shadow behind the face, were wings. Lena glanced down. A lion's body. Louder than a cat, at least. Her gaze darted back. She could just make out the scorpion's tail—or perhaps she imagined it, knowing that the manticore had to have one.

"Man flesh!" it roared, turning its face toward her. Its gray eyes did not look downward, or even focus on anything, but its nose wrinkled as it sniffed at the air.

Lena tore her gaze away and scrambled as fast as her feet could carry her toward the only passageway too narrow for a lion. Her heart hammered. She had come in search of a lion, she had found one—why had she been fool enough to try this venture? Hadn't the snake warned her that she pushed her knowledge too far? That escaping its poison should not send her in search of other monsters?

"Man flesh!" The manticore bounded forward—even a lion's soft feet struck with force enough to echo—and Lena scrambled up the stairway with the wind of its leap striking her in the back.

The walls shuddered with the force of its collision. One spat out bricks. The manticore roared, wordlessly, and the racket resounded in the passage. Lena, half-deafened, scrambled up and onward, and found herself facing a brick wall both more pale and more ruddy than those to either hand—as if newer—but mortared solidly in place. She bit her lip. And nowhere in her climb had there been a door, to either side.

She forced her breath in and out, and looked up. The light could not reach the ceiling wrapped in shadow. If she had only kept the rope, she might have escaped upwards. Perhaps. Her mouth twisted—if!

The manticore roared again.

She swallowed. Not truly a lion, she knew. All travelers' tales agreed on that, whatever other extravaganzas they proclaimed. A lion, thwarted of its prey, would seek out another rather than starve. It felt no outrage at escape—wasted no time lurking, vengefully seeking a chance to strike down the beast, or man, that escaped.

Lena looked slowly about. Then, carefully, she picked her way back to where the loose bricks lay. She put down the sundrop to free her hands. Once she had taken a brick up, she hesitated, but the manticore already gathered to lunge against the wall again. More bricks could fall, on her. She urged the light forward with her foot, to see that her shadow did not fall over her aim.

Then, her heart hammering, she hefted it up and hurled it over the manticore's shoulder. The brick soared out, brushing one bat wing.

The manticore did not turn, let alone pursue it.

Lena scrambled back. Her stomach roiled with the horror. It could trap her here until she died of thirst—and its blind face tracked her, somehow, as she moved.

Her hands clutched her skirt. After a minute, slowly, she took off her mantle. If it could see without seeing, she would give it a semblance more like hers.

She took up another brick to wrap in one corner, and make the mantle easier to throw. When the manticore crouched, ready for another pounce, she hurled it over the thing's head.

The tail whipped, faster than a falcon's strike, to pierce the mantle—and through, to its own hide.

It screamed in agony and convulsed. Lena snatched up the sundrop again and scrambled back as it thrashed, and thrashed, and thrashed. Bricks flew, and Lena cowered against the wall, clutching her light to herself. Fantastic shadows whirled, as if the wall were about to collapse and engulf her entirely.

Slowly, the sounds slackened, enough so she could hear her pounding heart—but a final blow might overcome the battered walls.

She forced her breath in and out. The walls might yield after the manticore died. Best to flee as soon as the manticore could not strike. At that, the guards had to have heard the ruckus.

Though they would know it was not her, they might come to see what roused it.

She began to inch forward.

Boots echoed against stone. She seized her sundrop and plunged it away again. In the gloom, she looked away, into the corner, drawing her headdress about. She would not see a soldier coming, but her face was most likely to betray her. She did not think she was so pale they would take her for a ghost.

Indistinct shouts followed. She could hear only the surprise, and then the hammer of running feet.

A hiss of shock followed. "Her mantle—it's here."

"You saw her close enough to know her mantle?"

"You saw her close enough to know *her*? What other fool woman would be down here, to leave a mantle?" He pulled back, by the sound of his footsteps. "At least she's dead." He snorted. "And out of sunlight. Serves her right, fool Celestian."

"Should bring the mantle. Only thing that shows—"

The other one snorted again. "Should report back. And we won't if that poison kills us both."

"Captain won't like it—" said the other, but without much fervor. And the sound of footsteps receded.

Sweat beaded on Lena's face, and trickled down. Her heartbeat hammered out the minutes, and finally, she peeked over her shoulder in the silence. No light could be seen. With care, and little speed, she uncoiled herself, and her stiff limbs slowly yielded. Nothing stirred in response to the noise. She straightened and drew out the sundrop. It flooded over the brick, and nothing stirred while she blinked.

The walls might yet fall, she reminded herself.

At the opening, the manticore sprawled. It had smashed its stinger against the wall, and a pool of poison—bright green, smelling acrid—had trickled from it, and sent rivulets over the floor. Her mantle lay stained with poison. For a moment, her hands snatched at air, but she could not risk it, not when the poison might work at a touch. She would look a fool, distraught and out of her wits, on the street, if she ever managed to rise up from this labyrinth.

She forced herself to set her mouth. She would once again look a fool. She had already risked a manticore and the king's guard. Looking a fool would not kill her.

She still felt exposed as she crept down the corridors and their cool, dank air.

At least, no other lights glinted from the brickwork. The guards must have quickly found their fellows and told them how she had succumbed to the manticore. Shadows loomed, and she forced her breath in and out. What could be down here? The manticore would have eaten it. . . .

Except that the manticore had not looked starveling. It had found enough to eat among these brick walls. She doubted that many men or women were as foolish as she was, to wander down here, so it was not that.

And the longer she lingered, the more time the creatures would have to find her.

Her footsteps resounded with her brisker pace, and she eyed each looming stone. It would serve her right, if she lost track of her path, in all her pondering of soldiers and what the manticore ate than the way. She could only hope that she did not wander here until Erion's reign ended in his strangulation.

It loomed before her: a stone carved with a gnarled tree, one she had seen before, carefully sketched. She surged forward, the sight of it freeing her like the break in a dam to the water within, and snatched herself up a moment before she touched it. Care, care, care—the first carved stone she saw should not overturn her wits when any trap set here could destroy her and all her hopes, and leave Erion no fate but death. Holding up the light in a hand that trembled, Lena counted the limbs to either side. At the end, she knew she had not mistaken the way. She sent her hand out

again, to lay it flat against the cool stone of the trunk. The carver
had even made it rough as bark. . . .

Moments inched by. Lena contemplated how years might
destroy more things than paper and cloth, how delicate spellwork
could perish, when rock groaned beneath her fingers, like a tree
in high winds. The stone shifted backward, to reveal itself a
door. She waited, her heart pounding, and heard no noise
within, once the door stopped. She looked in, at the stone
passageway that ran parallel to it.

It held no dust on a flag-stoned floor.

This, Lena reminded herself, was not the treasury of some
long-lost kingdom, buried beneath the weight of years. People
came and went here; perhaps only Erion's kingship, and so the
lack of decrees, kept her from meeting them here.

She straightened. That also meant that the traps could not be
too dangerous for those who knew the way.

She stepped inside. The door slid shut, with a puff of wind
that barely tweaked her skirt, and left her in air curiously
scentless. She turned left and walked onward.

A man sat ahead, and her heart leapt and hammered before
she realized that they had not set a guard here. The figure was
too large. Too uniformly pale, even its clothing. Too
unmoving—though, as she crept closer, she doubted that would
last. No man would leave a fine sculpture here for no reason.
And she had read of some of the enchantments, though not
detailed enough to mention this.

The light in her hand illuminated the statue, enough to show
it carved of white marble. Something glittered blue on its
forehead. Something enchanted. For beauty, they would never
have used blue, even hidden in the treasury, and so it had to be
for use.

The statue stood. As easily and deftly as a hale young man
standing, without any show of stiffness, and it held the sword

before itself. Its voice was deep and resonant, holding only the softest traces of inhuman stoniness.

"Who comes?"

All or naught, thought Lena.

"The king's betrothed wife. She comes to bring forth what is needed to preserve his life and his reign."

Her voice's echoes faded away. Madness, madness. King Halis had let superstitious fears, and yet more superstitious hopes, run away with him. Only a madwoman would trust her life to the web of lies he had woven to defend himself from imaginary dangers. That mockery of a coronation could make no king. . . .

The sapphire flared as white as the sun behind the thinnest of clouds—too brilliant to look upon. The statue stepped back and lowered its sword. For a moment, Lena dreamed of ordering it to let no one else in, but the danger of that order betraying her was too great. And she doubted that any of King Halis's servants would remember to speak of him as the king that was, or that the statue would permit their entrance even if they did. It was, after all, the king's treasury.

The statue saw nothing of her pondering. Its other hand reached to pull on a door that seemed heavier than the city gates, but whispered open beneath his grasp. From the first glimpses of the gloom within, jewels or gold or polished steel grabbed the light and sent it winking back at her. Nothing could be made out clearly, however much she peered. And not all of that gleamed white, she realized. Too much of it shone red for it all to be ruby, or glossy copper.

She realized, suddenly, that the statue had turned its stony face toward her, as if it ask whether she had lied, and had only come to gawk. It hardly mattered whether it opened the door, if she did not go within.

She strode forward. The pool of light about her lapped outward. Farther off things took up the glitter, and nearer things took on shape.

A gust of wind from behind her told her that the door closed as silently as it had opened. Lena drew her breath in and out—she should be glad of the security—and inched forward again. The nearest gleam was a tower of golden ingots, neatly stacked. More stood behind it, row and row. To either side, great chests stood, filled with heaps of gold coins, handy for payments.

The glow lay behind. From where she stood, the arched doorway was clear, and just a hint of the chamber beyond. She headed toward it. It was not as if she could bribe the guards for Erion's freedom with mere gold.

And if the king proved to keep salt here, why, she would merely remember that it denoted Erion's hospitality.

The ruddy glow increased with each step. From the echoes, a large room lay beyond—large enough to hold a king's ransom. She slowed as she approached, but not to stopping, until she reached the doorway.

All within was ablaze: suits of armor, both gilt and bejeweled; gold and silver ingots stacked into enormous towers; gowns and robes of satin set with gems; swords and spears and shields, all arrayed with richness. Gemstones heaped up like peaches or plums from a splendid harvest, and were resplendent in the fiery glow.

Slowly, she looked up, her neck arching. Hanging over all was a net woven, perhaps, from gold—it glittered—and caught in its mesh, the ruby she sought, enormous, perfect, glowing like a live coal.

Far, of course, from anything that a lone maiden could reach it from. Coins, and even ingots, the kings left where they could be fetched out, but the Lion's Heart, they wanted kept as the lamp in the treasury. She wondered for a moment whether she could throw the knife here. Then she wandered farther. She had known that, of course, that was why she had sought for the rope.

You could carry out enough gold to bribe half the city, an errant thought told her. Pile after pile of gold gleamed at her.

She reminded herself that nothing here, or even in the wildest legend, would ensure that they stayed bribed.

Lena walked father into the room. Her own light looked green in her hand when she glanced at it, but where its glow reached, gems and cloth showed moon pale, leaf green, the blues and purples of evening dusk. Even ingots looked like ripe wheat and not touched with fire, where their stacks towered, holding the gold that they did not expect to spend. She glanced up one heap. Over it, the fiery web gleamed.

Her gaze traced the fire back to its source, where the ruby glowed. She looked back at the ingots, stacked in a lattice. Then, slowly, she drifted back to the clothes. They were made of the very finest stuff, and laden with enchantment in every inch, to last this long.

Many minutes later, they lay heaped between two of the ingot towers. She sat on a chest, catching her breath, and hearing her heart pound. It would help little if she fell far, but it might muffle the ruby's drop. And it put the garments to more use than they had seen for many a year.

She glanced up at the ruby and carefully stowed the sundrop by the chest. She might need it again, but not to climb. After a minute, she went over to the plainest of the mantles, dyed a dark blue. They were not the rope, but the cloth was sturdy. Diamonds blazed along the hems, but nothing that a minute with the knife could not cut off. When the diamonds clattered to the floor, she set one newly plain mantle aside, to serve as her mantle in the street, and distract notice from her. The other fit neatly over her shoulders, and she eyed the ingots again.

What a fool. She rushed forward. Erion had days, but if she dispirited herself, he would need weeks and months for her to regain her courage.

The lattice gave her places to put her feet, but little grip for her hands. The metal was cold and slick wherever she touched it, and everywhere she could grasp it, shadows obscured her vision.

At least, she could slip her hands between them and hook the cross-wise ingots, though it squeeze her fingers to fit.

She took care not to glance downward.

Scrambling on top gave her one unsettling glance of far below. She crouched on all fours like a beast. Her eyes screwed shut, she fought, swallowing, to quell her stomach. She could not cower here when she needed to fetch down the ruby.

She opened her eyes and stared at the gold before her, ignoring the depths of the lattice. The ingots were spread far apart enough to make her footing dangerous. Moments later, she drew a deep breath and stood. The gold was steady under her feet.

The net gleamed with ruddy light, and she could gauge the distance between the tower and the stone. She would need to stretch but—she took out the knife—overhead, not to one side. Perhaps they had first built these towers to give them aid to suspend the net, using the gold just as they used the ruby to light the treasury while they kept it safe. They had to have gotten the net up here somehow.

After succeeding, she told herself, she might find an account in the library.

She straightened to her full height, reached up, and snagged the nearest cord. Harsh and metallic in her grip, it yielded not at all to her fingers. Only a faint tremor ran though the web. The light did not so much as tremble.

Lena brought up the knife. The cord did not yield to it, either. She set her mouth and began to saw. The cord shuddered, trembled, and began to fray. Lena hacked onward.

Slowly the cord succumbed, until, with a jump, the knife sliced into air, jolting her.

She released the cord. The net did not sink. She turned to the next.

Minutes inched by as cord after cord gave way. For a time, she wondered whether she could have to crawl within the net, over the open air, to fetch it, and her stomach felt cold, but slowly, as the cords broke, the net sagged, and the ruby shifted toward her. The distance shrank with every cord, and finally, she crept to the edge of the tower to put her hands about the jewel. The facets felt strange in her hands, if its being neither coal-hot nor cold were unnatural. She urged the ruby over the last strands and took it as it tumbled into her hands; it was large enough to be awkward even using both of them.

The ruby glowed in her arms—through her hands, adding a new ruddiness from the blood. Even her sleeves were not thick enough to contain the light. She took a step backwards and sat, with it glowing in her lap and her mouth drier than a desert.

Long minutes later, her heart's frantic beat having slowed, she thought—down. The Heart of the Lion did little good in the arms of the king's betrothed. None at all, if she sat there rather than went onward. She took up the stray mantle and went to wrap the ruby in it. It fit easily. Shadows thickened about the room, though rays of light still lay rosy in the air. Her sundrop's white light could be seen—faintly. She eyed the descent and thought of bearing this burden on her back.

After a moment, she pulled out the knife again. The mantle was long, and cutting with the grain produced long stripes that could be bound tightly first about the cloth wrapping the ruby, and then to each other until she had a long rope of cloth. Then, slowly, slowly, she lowered the ruby over the edge and eked out each inch of cloth as it sank, the cord pulling at her finger.

And then—it felt hours later—she added inches to the cord and felt it go slack. Her shoulders slumped.

It took another minute before she tried to look about—not easily, in the new gloom. Still, she could feel the cold, hard gleam of ingots, and she knew how long the descent was. Wrapping the cord about the ingots, several times, and knotting with more knots than sailors binding the king's barge against a storm, meant that she could yank on it, quite hard, and feel no yield.

She sat back on her heels. Descending would have been harder, even had the light not changed.

And if she frightened herself out of it, she would die of thirst while Erion still lived.

Before she could think farther, she scrambled to the side, and wedged a foot in the first foothold. It would be no harder than descending rocky slopes with a waterstone, she told herself, and wished she had not. Summoning up memories of lurching descents that had left her heart hammering—and how Erion had been there to steady her, as he was not here—

The Master of Heavens guides my feet as he guides the stars in their courses, she told herself, and searched out the next foothold with her other toes.

The descent was dizzying. Her own shadow, cast upward by both lights, dancing and whirled on the ragged surface of the tower. Once, her foot slipped, and she clutched her cord, certain that it would fray and break. Only with difficulty did she force her foot back. The gold seemed slicker with every step. Finally, she glanced down, gauged the distance, eyed the footholds—and jumped. She landed with a jolt and fought for her breath for an insanely long time for a woman who had triumphed. And once her breath had been mastered, she realized how her heart hammered.

Still, once her heartbeat steadied again, she collected her sundrop. By its whiteness, she took up her other mantle and donned it, to look fitting on the street. The broach was stiff and would not fasten properly, no matter how she poked it, but, she decided, the mantle looked passable enough. Anyone who looked closely enough would already be alert to the strangeness of her. She gathered up the ruby, cradling it like a baby, and walked toward the door.

It bore no door knob—as if she could push it open herself—but a brass bell stood to one side. Lena rang it. A deep, pure note pervaded the room. She put both her arms about the ruby again, and waited. The echoes died off into silence. Then, slowly, the door began to open.

The statue, sword in hand, faced her. The gemstone had turned blue again.

She could boldly step forward as if it made no matter that it stood there, or she could boldly declare—

"The king has need of this that I carry, with all haste."

Her voice rang, without even a hint of tremor. The stone flared white again. The statue did not move.

"No, he does not," came its stony voice. "No good king has need of that. No good king desires that. It brings shame and ignominy on the kingdom. It keeps the the king from defending its prosperity and pride—"

It spoke. It did not move to stop her. Lena took a step forward.

The statue strode to stand in her way. The sword swept upward.

She turned and fled before the blade rose over her head. In the treasury's clutter, she might stand a chance, like a rabbit among briars when the wolf pursued. Moments later, as if the statue took that long to realize that she had fled backward, its footsteps thundered after, drowning the sound of hers. She darted about the first tower of ingots and plunged her light away in a pouch. With it muffled, the room's only light was the stray gleams that escaped her bundle and turned the room into a morass of shadows and lurid gleams.

And betrayed her to pursuit. Even the masses of reflections could not wholly hide the source. But if she dropped it now, all had been in vain.

She scurried onward, past the towers, to where the chests stood. There she hesitated. Fleeing about the room might let her escape to the door, still open, but the statue could pursue her down the hall. And through the tunnels. And even in the city streets. Until weariness felled her, no doubt. Or the guards did.

She whirled to face the statue and hugged the ruby closer. Dropping it might make it think she yielded, and it might let her go, then. To never return. To have no way to rescue Erion.

The statue charged toward her, its sword rising. She waited, and waited, and her heart hammered out the moments until the sword began to fall.

She threw herself aside, and the floor's stones hit like a blow. Only through the thud and the tearing sound did she know the sword had struck. When she scrambled up, the statue already wrestled with the blade, trying to draw it from the chest.

She had no reason to believe it would wrestle forever, and its bare hands could kill. She drew out her sundrop. Whiteness engulfed the room again, letting her see the door clearly, and the struggling statue as well.

She scrambled toward the door. The statue gave a great heave, and the chest shifted, and Lena realized that the man and the sword were one, carved from a single stone. The blade had not been added. The statue could no more abandon its sword to chase her than it could abandon its hand.

And the door already started to shut behind her. King Halis might never reach his treasury again.

And serve him right, though Lena.

After a giddy minute, she put down her burden to straighten her mantle and her headdress. Looking less like a madwoman would let her get to the lion itself.

Even if she were a madwoman. She looked at the violet cloth swathing her and wished she had told tales of a violet-clad ghost woman, and claimed to have learned them in the library. That would scare them off. She smiled, feeling reckless and fey.

Light seeped into the tunnel. Daylight, but revealing little more of how much time had passed. It could not have been days, or she would have collapsed of thirst and hunger and weariness, she told herself. She hurried. If she remembered the way aright, the square outside held a clock.

And, it turned out, not many people. None of them looked toward her doorway, and she emerged into cloudy day. Hours had passed, but she still had hours until sunset. She fought down the urge to straighten her clothes and instead scurried along the street, holding the ruby tightly. Light would betray them, but a woman carrying a small package, even with great care, had obviously just returned from a merchant.

She had walked around seven corners and down scores of blocks, and up two flights of stairs, when a gasp made her start.

"Lena?" Anila scrambled up and seized her arm. "Lena, are you mad?" She gawked—at the clothes, Lena thought, not the bundle. Then she had a bundle of her own; their mother had sent her off with the laundry. Lena could even see her own garments in Anila's arms.

"What else should I be in a city of madness?" said Lena. Passersby started to glance at them; her heart hammering, she swept Anila off to an alleyway. They could not talk long, but having Anila on her heels would be worse. She tried to steady her breath.

"Soldiers are everywhere," said Anila. "And we don't own that mantle. And you're so near the palace."

"It hardly matters where I am," said Lena, but felt her heart hammering still harder. "If they are *everywhere*. Besides, this is also close to the—erstwhile king."

Anila's eyes widened.

"I'm even nearer to the evening house." Lena leaned forward. "And so are you. Laundry must be done, short of the heavens falling, but—why oh why do you come so close in these times? Here—"

Lena looked about and picked out one niche. There, she laid aside her bundle, took a headdress and a gray mantle from Anila's, and changed in the gloom.

"There. Bundle these up, all together, and no one will see it." Lena snatched up her own bundle. "Tell people that, yes, a strange woman clad in violet stopped you and questioned you about the evening house in a vengeful manner."

"In an old dress, like a ghost of years ago," said Anila, thoughtfully.

Lena smiled. An excellent grasp of it—

Anila spread her feet and braced herself. "Not without seeing what you've got in there."

Lena thought of pushing by her.

Anila drew herself up to her full height, tilted her head back to look down her nose, and said in what was no doubt the loftiest tone she could manage, "It might be wrong to aid you. My sister Lena would rebuke me for helping you without even trying to learn. That's the way you end up doing wrong, and in trouble—"

Strangling Anila would attract too much attention. Even back here, a ruckus would draw eyes.

So would a shriek.

"If you make a peep," said Lena, "you will pay for it with your life."

She must have managed an ominous tone: Anila took a step backwards, her eyes widening. Lena shifted the bundle to show just a hint of the light.

Color drained from Anila's face. She took another step back and stared at Lena's face. Her mouth worked, but not even a peep emerged. Lena wrapped up the ruby again.

"You—you—" Anila's voice was low—low enough to draw no guards—but filled with horror. "You robbed the king. That's magic. Only the king—"

"Don't be foolish," said Lena tranquilly. "I am the king's betrothed. I brought it out for Erion's benefit, as it is his for so long as he is king."

Anila's eyes widened farther than Lena had realized they could go. "They won't care if they catch you."

"All the more reason to divert them," said Lena. "Tell them about a strange woman in purple who concerned herself with the evening house."

Anila still stood without twitching.

Lena leaned forward and whispered, "And afterward, I will tell you how I did it."


It had helped, Lena supposed, as she walked down more streets, that Anila had looked like a girl who had seen a ghost. A woman in purple—half the people about her talked of that woman. Her mouth tightened as she came around a corner. They had not gossiped so when Erion had been chosen for king.

Then, Erion was a mere scholar, not a ghost.

Soldiers pressed by her, not noticing how she shrank back farther than prudence needed. At a booth, they seized the Solarian woman there, upsetting her stacks of headdresses over the flagstones and demanding to know these tales of this purple woman.

"I thought I saw her," Lena called. All the buyers and sellers stared at her. More slowly, the soldiers, their grips slackening on the woman, turned toward her, and their eyes narrowed. She pointed out a suitable street. "There. Heading toward the evening house."

Moments later, the woman scrambled to retrieve her wares before they were all trampled.

If only all of the guards converged that easily, Lena thought, as she walked onward, the other way. She would find it simple to make her way—at last, something simple. Perhaps it was only fitting that something be simple for once, finally.

Soldiers appeared, stalking along the street. One eyed Lena, and she started.

Before they could wonder why, she blurted out, "The woman in purple. I saw her—there." She pointed.

She watched their backs for a moment. It was even true. Her mouth twisted, and she hurried on. She had seen herself if not her face. Just as she had walked toward the evening house before she walked past it.

She directed another set of soldiers away from there before she reached a square where a statue of a lion stood, towering from the height of the stairs. Carved from ruddy golden stone, it posed with its mouth perpetually opening to roar. Crowds, bustling about their business, streamed about it, not a soul giving it a glance. How many, after all, had ever heard of its legend? She had not, not before Erion had read it to her. She struck out, over the flagstones, wary for any passerby. It would not be clear until she came close, but to go anyway but around would draw eyes.

A swarm of soldiers, far more than she had misdirected, came down a broad avenue, as if advancing on a fortress. Lena hurried toward the statue; she was close enough to look as if she took refuge, trying to get out of their way.

It did not turn their gazes from her.

"The woman in purple—" she began.

"That's her," snapped one soldier. "The madwoman who's given us that merry chase."

Lena ran.  Three steps later, she knew she had betrayed all, but she could not stop.  Soldiers hammered after her as if nothing could deceive them.  One, pounding after, snagged her mantle.  She tried to pull free, and the stiff pin came loose, flooding him with cloth.  Thank the Master of Heaven and Earth that she had been unable to fasten it right.  She sprang up the steps and clambered onto the statue.  Her free hand reached out to snag a stony paw, and she climbed, the ruby a lump against her.

She picked out the carved hole, and a hand seized her foot.  She kicked.  The moment that bought her let her shove the ruby from its nest in the mantle, into the niche.  It landed with a dull thud.  Red light flowed from the niche, but otherwise it was as mute and motionless as any rock.

Hands seized her arms.  Her head jerked about to see soldiers had gotten firm footing before they seized her.  With ease, they swept her off the statue and hurled her to the hands of the soldiers below, whose grips were bruising.  About, the crowd murmured.

"Madwoman indeed," said one, contemptuously.

"Perhaps our king should have a queen," said another, with a sneer.

Lena waited, quietly, in their hands.  Even if she could have fought free, she had carried out what she intended.  The soldiers did not even try to retrieve the ruby.  And, as she stared up at the statue, she thought they had no need to do.  For each marvel she and Erion had found at the library and then outside, they had read of a dozen more legends that had never existed, or vanished without a trace, or been so confused in the telling that they could not know the source if they stumbled over it.

"What did she put in there?" said one deep voice.

The soldiers turned, their faces set in incredulous lines, toward the grizzled lieutenant who spoke.

"We got the madwoman—what does it matter what the madness had her carry about?"

"Mad to *care*," said another soldier.

"Look," said the lieutenant, and pointed. "It *glows*. Any madwoman who can do that—"

Soldiers hauled her to her feet, and two seized her arms. The others looked at each other as if holding a sorceress and madwoman were a pleasant task beside retrieving whatever she had put within. Despite herself, her mouth twitched. A petty vengeance, frightening them with an enchantment that did not harm. Still, it pleased her that none of them even looked at the statue. . . .

Its fur rippled. Lena swallowed. Its shoulders twitched, and its paws shifted. Her heart seemed to stop for a minute before it hammered in her chest. She had not despaired at her failure because she had not really believed anything possible.

The lion did not cease for her doubts. Its shoulders twitched, its paws shifted, and she felt her breath come light and fast. To actually see the lion of legend was more frightening that she had dreamed possible.

Beside her, a soldier grunted and looked up. Then he froze, his fingers rigid on her arm. The other one gasped, and a moment later, her arm was free as he edged away. The knowledge rippled through the soldiers, out to the crowd. Shrieks resounded, and then the hammer of footsteps in flight. Even some soldiers fled.

Lena pulled free of the soldier still holding her. All could be lost yet. She snagged her mantle where it had fallen, for some dignity, and strode forward.

The statue's—the lion's—eyes opened. Slowly, its head bent so that it looked into the square, and Lena met its gaze. Behind her, the last and bravest of the soldiers fled, after the crowd. Lena swallowed. She had put a deep trust in the truthfulness of the books she had read, to stand here so steadily.

Then, no one would protect her from King Halis, if the lion did not.

Its deep voice rumbled, as if ready to shake the city's foundation stones. "Where is the king?"

"I will bring you to him," said Lena, pulling on the mantle.

Its shoulders bunched, and its words were growled. "Why is he not here?"

"His enemies prevent it. Set by the king—"

The lion frowned.

"—that was," said Lena, hastily. "The erstwhile king. The king who abdicated of his own free will and compelled another to assume the crown, and yet would hold the king's power as if he had not."

The frown eased.

"I am the king's betrothed wife. I will lead you to him."

The lion's head descended in a solemn nod. Then it rose again, and higher than it had before, to roar.

Lena's hands clapped over her ears. Buildings about trembled. The last souls, bold enough to gawk until this, fled.

The lion leap down, making the street shake, leaving Lena surprised that the flagstones did not crack. She forced her breath in and out, trying to steady herself.

"Which way?" it growled.

Mutely, Lena pointed. The lion surged forward, and she scrambled to keep up to her only protection. At the next crossing, it looked at her.

Instead of pointing, she drew a deep breath. "Once—we get close, we—may have to search—"

The lion nodded as gravely as a king out of legend, but Lena still led off, as swiftly as she had gone before, paying no heed to her breath.

Crowds had gathered. They murmured along the way, but the lion surging down the way, and the glances it gave, gave her a path clearer than she had ever had before through the city. Which was well, considering how swiftly she had to move.

The petitioners' hall, she thought. They even compelled petitioners—the poor, and Celestians—to present theirs to Erion. She wondered whether King Halis would void them all or consider them after. Or, rather, which he had meant to do.

But as that building loomed before them, in a yellowish beige stone with suns emblazoned on it to represent all-illuminating justice, a clump of men came down the steps: guards in their uniforms, and in the center, dressed more ornately than ever King Halis had been when receiving petitioners, Erion was manhandled along.

"There," called Lena, letting her voice ring. "See how his foes maltreat him."

The lion crouched, gathering itself, and bounded down the street. Lena gathered her skirts and ran after, unwilling to let it pass without her. If Erion did not realize—if he misspoke to the lion—

For all her short breath, she reached them while the lion loomed over all. Its eyes shifted to glance among them more swiftly than a songbird in flight. The soldiers seemed too frightened to flee, their mouths working silently. Lena thought some of them trembled. Erion, pale, looked at it. Then his gaze drifted to her, where she fought for her breath, and it was then that he started.

The lion's voice was deep and growling. "Who is the king?"

A minute later, the soldiers found strength enough to mutely point at Erion. The lion turned its face toward him, and its tail lashed. Moments inched by as it stood, its gaze intent on Erion, as still as if it had turned to stone again. Lena wondered—as her heart pounded—whether the legends had been wrong. Or, even if they were true, the kings had corrupted the enchantment, and the lion might devour Erion whole. And her, after.

The lion drew itself up to its full height to bow, its belly going down flat to the street. A moment after, Lena bowed as well, so deeply that she wonder that she kept her balance. But the lion must never think that Erion was anything less than king—her heart pattered faster than it had, running or facing down the armed sculpture.

Then the lion sat back on its haunches and roared again. It shook the air, and the soldiers staggered and fled. It roared on and on, as if not caring that it let the king's enemies flee justice.

Something moved on the wall's height. Lena glanced about. Lions—statues of lions—prowled about, gathering in a pride large enough to fill the square and overflow it.

The roar cut off abruptly enough that Lena felt deaf for a moment. Then all the lions bowed, and in such a mass that she could clearly hear their movements.

"You," rumbled the first lion, "are a just king, whom we may aid to rule in justice?"

"I shall strive to be," said Erion, gravely. "I am new to the throne, and my—councilors have done much to hinder me even thus far into my reign."

Lena let her breath out in a gasp of relief. Erion had guessed what she had done—knew what he had to do himself. She swallowed and tried to scold herself. Very few things indeed could have stirred up these lions of legend. Half the city had to have guessed what she had done, and those who had not—had yet to see the lions.

"Rubies," said the lion, with such distaste that Erion did not move, and Lena glanced anxiously over the rubies and topazes embroidered on his robe. "It was not the custom of just kings to wear gemstones that made them look blood splattered."

Lena felt a cold weight in her stomach. So that part of the legend was also true.

"A corrupt custom," said Erion smoothly. "Not, however, the worst of them, and so to be amended later, when time can be spared from injustices and injuries. Justice must be done. More, justice must be seen to be done, that all may know of it."

He looked over the pride of stony lions before him, and for a moment looked like a frightened boy-child.

"Three of you must come with me. The others must keep order in the city, as I can trust none of the soldiers who should obey me."

The lions bowed very low—to the king, Lena reminded herself, and bowed with them.

"Your Majesty, there was a guard on the treasury, but your enemies mastered it, so it does not guard as it ought to." She drew a deep breath. Erion seemed more shocked at her address than considering what to do next. "Let a lion guard it. I fear much gold will be needed, to spend and to cure what your enemies have done."

Erion blinked, but nodded. "Let one go, to guard the gold. As for you, my betrothed, my beautiful dove—" He smiled. "Come with me, as I go to face my enemy."

Her stomach felt cold and leaden. She bowed again, hiding her face. What had she thought would be done? Letting the king—Halis, she told herself—letting Halis go free could only leave them in danger. To dream that the lions' mere appearance would resolve all that they faced—did not befit a queen, Lena concluded. Even a merely betrothed one.

She walked meekly alongside Erion, a little behind as befit a subject, even one (her mouth twitched) of such high station. A trio of lions paced solemnly with them, either recognizing Erion's injuries or regarding haste as unbefitting to a king.

The crowds thickened so much that even with their escort, the people sometimes had trouble giving way. When shoves and scuffles broke out, the lions gave them baleful glances, and the crowds subsided into silence. Every now and again, roars resounded, some near, some far off. Lena could not be certain that all of them came from within the city. Her fingers tightened on her mantle.

"Much has changed, Your Majesty," the lion rumbled. "Passes to your kingdom have been opened, to the south and east." To the Solarian lands, thought Lena. The lion rumbled on. "Other have been closed, to the north and west." To Celestian lands.

Her heart pattered faster, and she glanced sideways at Erion. His face seemed lighter than moments before.

"I do not think their influence has been wholesome," said Erion, gravely. "Within a month, we shall open those that were closed. I must consider the open ones, whether they aid my subjects, but I do not doubt that I shall have several of them closed."

Sibilant whispers spread outward from them. Some of the nearest shifted a little forward, as if they wanted to appeal to the king, but then they pulled back. As the news spread through the crowd, some passersby paled, or started, or even turned to flee.

She whispered so to Erion.

He whispered back, "Evil has befallen the king. He must reign over a land where the greedy and powerful have done much to incite hatred and rage."

"And," murmured Lena, "the greedy can feign having suffered at their hands." Erion winced. She thought of how those who fled would be most marked by cowardice, but that matter they could leave to another day.

The crowds opened up before them. The evening house, in extravagant rosy-red stone, stood opposite them in the square. Its bronze front doors were set with suns in the sky. Erion strode toward it. Lena wondered whether they would have to hunt through its halls as if looking for a mouse, and whether the King—Halis—would flee, and if the lions could spread word of his appearance.

The doors opened, swiftly, silently. Against the room's looming darkness, Halis gleamed in cloth of gold. His jaw worked.

"That," said Erion, "is the king who was, who sets my authority at naught, though his sun has set, and mine is rising."

"You fool," said Halis. "You fool!" He raised his hands, showing a green gemstone as clear as any spring water. "Did you think that the true kings are such fools? To let the lions stand about the city so, when we would have no defense? That we did not know that taking out their heart did not mean it could not go back in?"

His gaze flickered back to the lions.

"You have imperiled the pride and glory of this realm, unleashing these monsters. But we are ready for you!"

The lions growled and crouched, ready to pounce.

"You will obey me!" Halis took a step forward. "Be still!"

A lion's tail, lashing across the cobblestones, froze as if the ruby had been removed, and taken all life with it. Gasps sounded from the crowd, and excited whispers.

Halis raised the stone higher. "Command the others to gather here!"

Nothing happened. Halis frowned, eyed the crowds, which started to murmur, and held the stone up the his fingers. "Command the others to gather here!"

The lions—remained still, Lena realized. Slowly, slowly, she put her hand toward the dagger. When her fingers slid around the hilt, she whipped it out and hurled it toward Halis. He started, and too late tried to snatch for the stone. It toppled from his hands to hit the cobblestones, and crack, the sound ringing from the stone about.

The lions roared and pounced. A moment later, Erion's arm slipped about her and pulled her close to him. She buried her face in his shoulder. She had not thought that far ahead—only to stopping him—and all that blood—but Erion could not have let him live, whatever happened.

Minutes later, the lion said, in a deep growl, "May all your enemies so perish, Your Majesty."

Lena pulled away. Erion looked very pale, but grave. The green gemstone showed only a little of its color, sitting in a pool of blood that trickled out farther, over the stones. And it was well that many had seen Halis come forth, and could swear to his death, because no man could lay a name to him now.

"I have many enemies, I fear," said Erion. "Many are within this castle."

A man came forward, gray-haired, gray-bearded, dressed in robes like a councilor. He bowed, deeply. "Your Majesty."

Erion scowled, as if trying to remember the man among the swarms of councilors who had urged the king onward. She could not, but she had never come close to the court.

"Much of the court locked themselves and above, in dread, as soon as the news came. They have few guards with them, but I fear that the stairs were built to withstand an assault. I know no way in."

Lena straightened. "I do. I must fetch it."


The rope of spider silk lay as lightly in her hands as it had before. Even Erion raised an eyebrow at it. The officials and guards who had emerged to hail Erion as king overtly stared at it. Some looked almost green, and glanced often at Erion.

"My gracious bride," said Erion—not glancing about, though he could not have chosen that strange address for her sake—"is it best that you use it, or should I have my soldiers do so?"

"Let your soldiers do so," said Lena. "Your Majesty."

Erion glance about and pointed out the tallest of them, with broad shoulders—one who looked uneasy, Lena noticed.

"Your Majesty." He edged forward but glanced between the two of them. "There is no grapple to it."

Lena held it out. "It is spider silk, and will hold in its own. They can neither cut it nor throw it back down."

But you, she thought, can climb it on your own. Enough trouble for me to get the ruby down. Someone else can do this.

The guard took the rope. A low buzz of talk sprang up, and Lena looked away.

"Lena!" Anila charged at her, and threw her arms about her waist.

"Anila!" rebuked Lena. "Is that any way to act before the king?"

There was an uncommon silence, and it seemed to Lena that every eye was on them. Anila sniffed, and stared about, not releasing her sister.

"In view of the danger you were in, my dear bride," said Erion, "sisterly devotion is reason enough for her neglecting it."

"But not for long," said Lena. Anila goggled, surprised enough to let Lena push her through bowing to Erion. And she added a whispered but stern injunction to keep silent before bundling her aside. Her heart pattered faster as the guard went to throw the rope. For an idle moment, she wondered if she and Anila should return home. They might be utterly useless here.

Then, she had not proved useless after Erion had been chosen as king.


The halls gleamed with gold and red and blue, flowers and birds and trees painted in intricate array. Anila's hand was clammy in hers, but not so cold as her stomach felt.

"In here, my dear bride."

Lena swallowed and walked into a room where the walls showed silver deer sporting among silver birches, but everyone clumped grimly about a niche in the back of the room.

"This," said Erion, pushing forward a dish where a flower had been ground into dust. "Have a care with it."

She scarcely had to hear that. A few petals had escaped crushing to reveal their form. She suppressed the urge to ask if he had foolishly touched it, and only said, "That is the black lotus."

"Black lotus?" said one guard. "There is no such thing as the black lotus."

Lena looked at him. "As there is no such thing as the lions."

A moan came out of the niche. Pulcherie, sprawled in disarray, looked out, but her eyes showed only black with the faintest rim of color.

"My love?" she said, plaintively. "My beloved king? He is well?"

"He—rests." Lena took a stride to reach the other woman, and found that her arm felt as cold as it looked. "Soon, you will join him."

Pulcherie smiled. "How well, how well—I could not bear it, you know, to wait in fear. So—it helped."

Behind her, Lena heard Erion giving order that she be attended until her death.

That would not take long. Lena let her breath out. Kudret had poisoned himself wittingly, and so had many others. She stared across the room, and it seemed very large, and she remembered that she was the king's betrothed wife. His queen would be expected to ensconce herself in such rooms.

With evening, the sun broke through enough to turn the western clouds into a flowery mead of scarlet, rose, and orange. On the steps of the evening house, Anila shifted her weight between her feet, like a small child wondering when things would be done. Lena could not blame her. She had never thought this far ahead. It seemed improper for the king's betrothed, that she just wound her way through the streets to her father's house. More, it seemed dangerous. But evening had arrived, and the air grew chilly.

"Lena!" Her mother hurried over the flagstones. "I heard—I heard tales—but—I didn't—" Her gaze went from Lena to Erion, to the lion. She only managed to tear her gaze away after a minute, to look mutely at the guards and officials paying court to Erion.

Anila grinned. Lena had never felt less like smiling in her life.

Bela puffed up, and eyed it all. "Shocking," she grumbled. "All the city will *ring* with scandal."

"Then there must be none," said Erion, his voice ringing. "It is well that you have come, Lady Mirjam, as evening comes. Best that my gracious and beloved betrothed and her dear sister return to their father's roofs."

Her mother bowed. "Your Majesty." Rising, she gave Bela a baleful, sideways glare. Slowly, Bela bowed as well.

"I will appoint a lion to watch over them during the night." One lion bowed to them. Erion, as if he had never dreamed of anything else, went on. "And to escort my betrothed lady to me again in the morning, for the Lady Lena's aid is needed. Many cases must be reviewed for injustice, and as she can read them and judge them justly, I will have need of her."

Bela started to mumble, too low for even Lena to hear.

Erion smiled. "The sooner that all is well, and the church properly consecrated to celebrate our wedding and her coronation, the sooner that happy day shall come."

For a fugitive moment, Lena thought of the library's being torn up, and cringed. Then she tried to shame herself: it was a church, and she had every reason to be grateful to the Master of Heavens. She glanced over at Erion. His gaze was steady on the great church of the Solarians. And—he had not spoken of *re*-consecrating it.

She tried not to be glad, but not very hard.  Bowing, she said, "I go as you command, Your Majesty, and will return as you command, as well."

Even as the streets darkened, and the smells of evening meals spread from kitchens, Lena could see the crowds had changed. They had walked down seven squares and about three corners before she could put her thumb on why, but then, she thought herself a fool.  More people sported scarves, or more, in blue, with stars and the moon on them.  For a moment, she fancied that Celestians had found new boldness already, but then she saw faces she knew.  She counted.  One Solarian might be a fool, or two, but dozens confirmed her thoughts.

"Blasted knaves," said Bela.  "Jumping to pass themselves off as Celestians."

"I am sure," said Lena, "that the king will not take such fraud lightly."  She sighed.  The king would have much to do, to ensure justice.


Anila stood in the doorway, looking at Lena.  "If *you* are going to be queen, what's going to happen to me?"

Lena's mouth twisted.  "I assure you, very few people have complained that they are sisters to queens."

"But I want to learn the library!  If Erion's king, and you're queen, there's no one to teach me!"  She leaned forward and whispered, "Aunt Bela told me I couldn't be a librarian."

Lena sighed.  She and Erion would find it hard to even consult the library, no doubt.  Perhaps they could devise some way to have her taught.

But the kingdom had to come first.

Along the streets, lions prowled. Great houses had their doors sealed with the king's insignia, proof that all within was forfeit, because the family had fled rather than face King Erion's justice.

People also moved about. Fewer, and more quietly, than Lena had ever seen before. And the blue scarves were yet more plentiful.

Lena, the lion, and Anila crossed the square. The lion walked with imperial calm, surveying all that appeared before it, majestically indifferent to those who gawked, and those who fled in terror, and those who made a low reverence to the king's betrothed and left her path with swiftness.

In a month or two, Lena thought, she would take those bows as only her due. And the easy path through the city.

At the church doorway, the great bronze doors were down. Artisans bent over them, with new panels, adding blue to the gold, and silvery stars and moons.

Lena walked on, feeling more unsettled. Her fingers came up to trace the stars on her scarf, and she pressed nearer the lion.

Guards escorted her within the castle, despite their uneasy glances at the lion, to an audience chamber where Erion sat enthroned, attended by half a dozen lions. His robes were blue and silver—and how the seamstresses of the city must have rummaged through their stores of cloth, and sewn all night, to dress him so!—and petitioners knelt before him. Scarves of blue and silver lay before the throne, mute witnesses against them.

Lena made her bow. Erion made no more than a hand gesture to acknowledge it, but his gaze met hers, and he smiled, so faintly that only she could have seen it.

"Grandmother insisted on it," said the oldest man there, his hair laced with white. "That we were Celestians who had hid ourselves when our eyes became dark."

Lena's eyebrows went up. A new excuse to evade the fines then. She glanced about and spotted the sapphire from the statue, retrieved from the treasury. It had not turned black, but it had darkened.

She pulled back into the Queen's Niche, ushering Anila with her. A chair had been set out for her, and a little table with paper, pen, and ink. Apparently advice to the king could be discreet. But she sat—Anila plopped on the floor—and reached for her sewing bag. Listening to audiences meant she could not read lawsuits at the same time, but a new scarf for the king lay in her powers. She and Anila were both at work before the petitioner stopped his plea.

"This tale can hardly please me," said Erion. "To have such subjects, who disown the Master of Heavens for cowardice and advantage? What hope has a mere king for their loyalty?"

Mumbled denies, and claims of devotion to their grandmother, followed. Lena appraised their clothes. If they had not done it for advantage, yet it had done them no harm. She took another stitch. If they even told the truth at all. They started to furiously disown any claims of having done it for greed.

"I shall take you at your word," said Erion, regally. "You shall pay a fine for having concealed your allegiance, and everyone shall know it was not for advantage."

For a moment, their faces contorted, but they glanced at the lions serenely flanking Erion. They bowed and murmured of their gratitude, and his gracious clemency.

Lena bent her head over the sapphire-colored cloth. She wondered how many would claim to have been dark-eyed Celestians, and whether any would be telling the truth. It was a moment later when Anila poked her, and Lena realized how wide-eyed her sister was.

Rodvan bowed before the throne. Her needle froze in midair. Rodvan's son bowed as deeply as his father—more so. Though she thought Rodvan looked the more frightened. When he knew Erion. . . .

"You come shame-faced," said Erion.

"And why should I not? One among our number, admitted to the library, set the guards upon your fair and wise betrothed as she sought out the Lion's Heart. It could have been me, I knew she was about something, I appealed to her to cease—" His hands spread.

Lena's mouth was dry.

"Did you set them?" said Erion, coldly.

"No, Your Majesty. But what reason have you to believe me?"

Lena glanced over. Erion glanced down. The sapphire was snow-white, though it did not shine, and reveal the king's secrets.

"Peace, good Rodvan. A king shall not do injustice because it might prove justice, if only he knew what he does not." His mouth twitched. "You must have much feared my wrath, to petition so."

"No, Your Majesty, that is not the import of my petition." Rodvan straightened. "I told you that I appealed to the Lady Lena your betrothed to cease her madness and preserve her life. There is no way she could have succeeded, a mortal maid alone."

Erion cocked an eyebrow.

Rodvan blinked and looked like a stubborn owl caught in daylight and unwilling to retreat.

"Only the Master of Heavens could have guided her steps so, when she walked so far underground."

The needle slid from Lena's fingers.

"I wish to become a Celestian, and my son with me."

Lena slowly lifted her head to stare. He would not be alone, there would be many like him in the city and in the land, but for him, and him alone, she wondered at his purpose.

Erion sat as still as stone.

She bit her lip. As a queen, perhaps she should wonder what Erion might do, being king. To forbear, to let Rodvan pass without forfeit, because they knew him, because they trusted his intentions—would it be just? Even if it were, would it only cause discontent in the city, that one wriggled so easily to a place of advantage? Erion's new reign was not secure, and justice must be seen to be done.

A minute later, Lena seized the pen and began to write. A quick-learning page boy appeared by her hand before she was half done. Either he or her writing drew Erion's eye, and silence continued until the boy's footsteps pattered over the stones.

Erion read, swiftly, and looked up.

"It has taken you long to realize his providence," he said solemnly. "And whoever now realizes it, must pay a price, to show his sincerity. Of you, I shall demand a service."

Rodvan bowed, hiding his face.

"You shall instruct Lady Anila, my betrothed's sister, in the matters of the library. Without fee or gift."

After a moment, Anila clapped her hand to her mouth to keep from squeaking like a mouse. Nothing could stop her wriggling. Lena smiled and sewed on. The reign of King Erion— the Just, no doubt—would show more clemency than King Hallis's had.

The lions looked pleased. Her smile deepened. Then, with what they had done for Erion, the lions had pleased her; it was only just to make return.

# Also by Mary Catelli

Curses And Wonders
Dragon Slayer
Eyes of the Sorceress
Fever and Snow
Mermaids' Song
Sword and Shadow
The Book of Bone
Witch-Prince Ways
Dragonfire and Time
Enchantments And Dragons
Jewel of the Tiger
Over the Sea, To Me
The Dragon's Cottage
The Maze, the Manor, and the Unicorn
The White Menagerie
A Diabolical Bargain
Madeleine and the Mists
Magic And Secrets
The Lion and the Library
The Princess Goes Into The Forest
The Wolf and the Ward
The Witch-Child and the Scarlet Fleet
Treachery And Spells
Winter's Curse
Crow Curse
Free Passage
Isabelle and the Siren
Journeys And Wizardry
Lifestone

Magic of the Lost God
Never Comment On A Likeness
One Name
The Drunken Mermaids
The Turtle in the Sea of Sand
Were I You
Where There Is Smoke